PIECES OF EIGHT

MELISSA WRIGHT

THE FREY SAGA

PIECES
of EIGHT

MELISSA WRIGHT

PIECES
of EIGHT

THERE WERE ONLY THREE CERTAINTIES IN MY NEW LIFE.

The first was that I couldn't be certain of anything. The bonds that kept me from my memories hadn't been fully undone. The shattered images from before the binding didn't fit together the way they should have. I had tried to force them, but my bonds held me from reconciling the two lives: the years I'd lived as a dark elf, strong and powerful, and the more recent part—the part that seemed more real—where I'd been trapped, living as an untalented, unmagical light elf.

There weren't many memories of the first years, the ones spent in the castle where I was born, in line for the throne. Most of the information I had about that life came from reading my mother's diary after she was gone. The few memories that returned later were scattered. Attached to them was a feeling of strength, a power and confidence that was nothing like my second life.

For all that time, I'd thought I was a graceless light elf, an outcast, unable to use magic, but it turned out that my magic had been taken from me. I was still ungraceful, but at least I had a few special talents all my own. Not that I could even think about where that left me. My power and lineage would put me at the head of the dark elves' realm.

Everything I'd known had been proven false, and I was still struggling with reassembling the broken pieces.

The bits that *did* fit were my new family, the seven other elves who had fought to save me. We had only spent a short time together, but I had become dependent on them—honestly, I had been dependent on them all along but simply hadn't known it. They'd protected me from Council, who had bound me from magic and stolen my memories. Council, who had burned my mother and wanted to burn me.

"Frey."

Focus. I had a bad habit of getting lost in my thoughts. It was confusing there, foggy.

Ruby cleared her throat.

"I'm listening," I insisted, shaking out my hands to ready myself for another assault.

"We have to continue your training, Frey. It's important."

I narrowed my gaze on Ruby, not convinced my safety was really the issue. I had my suspicions that she enjoyed the training more than she let on. But Chevelle had insisted, and they'd been working with me daily since I'd woken in the castle with my memories partially restored. He'd assured me it was not a good idea to reveal that my bonds were still in place, for my own protection. I'd barely seen him in the days since we'd arrived.

Ruby's whip cracked beside my head.

Grey, who had a tendency to drop by on the days I trained with Ruby, chuckled at my expression, moving to stand. "Give her a break, Ruby," he said. "Frey, why don't you rest for a bit, go get something to eat?"

I didn't miss the glance she shot him. I waited, hoping she would agree.

"Fine." She waved a dismissal, bracelets clinking at her wrist.

I hurried to the door, wanting to make my escape before she changed her mind, but I had to turn back. My fingers played over the leather of my new breastplate. "Ruby?"

Though I'd been there for weeks, I still got lost any time I tried alone to traverse the maze of corridors. With an exaggerated sigh, she pointed me in the right direction.

"Thanks," I said over my shoulder, not giving her a second chance to stop me. The castle was massive, and that section of corridor was wide enough to accommodate a half-dozen men. I hung along the edge, feeling comfort in the closeness of the cool, dark stone, and tried to decide whether to eat in the dining area or just raid the pantries.

My steps were soft, the leather soles of my boots making no noise in the empty hall, so the echo of voices caught my ears well before I realized whose they were. I followed them, coming to rest outside a chamber a few doors down.

Chevelle saw me standing in the doorway and dismissed the slim, dark-haired man he'd been speaking with. The stranger—a castle guard, I thought—inclined his head as he passed me, his eyes skirting my own to follow the line of the floor. I waited, watching Chevelle as the sound of the man's steps receded. Chevelle had always been striking with his strong jaw, dark hair, and eyes of the deepest blue, but there was something more there too. Lingering at the back of my mind was some half-remembered dream I couldn't quite pull into focus. Those hazy memories felt as if they wanted me to reclassify every single look, every momentary break in his expression, but they weren't truly my memories, not yet.

When the hall was finally silent and he could let down his defenses, Chevelle smiled at me. It was nothing out of the ordinary, simply the same greeting I received from any of my guard, but because it was him, I flushed. I always flushed when I saw him those days, whereas before, it had been sporadic. Before he'd thought I was her, Elfreda of North Camber instead of Frey from the village, when he'd thought I was *that* Frey and he'd kissed me. I fought the urge to touch my lips at the intensity of that remembered kiss, but it had only lasted a moment.

Because he'd realized I was not the forgotten girl inside of me.

I worked to push the thought away, but no matter how I tried, I couldn't. In fact, it was almost all I thought of with any kind of clarity.

The second thing I was certain of was that I wanted him.

The moment my cheeks colored, Chevelle's smile fell back into his standard, stern expression, and he asked, "Shouldn't you be training?"

My jaw flexed, and I pressed my palm against the carved stone framing the doorway. "They said I could take a break, get something to eat."

He nodded and went back to his work, and I turned from the room without another word. I sifted through my thoughts as I went, still trying to find some kind of order. Reaching out to trace the interlocking lines of the stone wall, cool and smooth beneath my fingertips, I let my steps slow to listen for echoes through the corridor.

I couldn't say what I was missing in the memories of Chevelle, what dark secrets our past held, or why he'd kept his distance until he'd thought me restored, but other memories called to me. The recent days of training seemed eerily familiar, and it wasn't just that some part of my mind recognized the practice rooms—the feeling of being forced, of being trapped, was something I had experienced before. I was stronger—there was no question of that—but I still wasn't fully in control. However, they all insisted that I be prepared for anything. They were worried about someone finding out I was weak, confused, and unable to lead.

I was in danger in my own home.

Fingers still trailing the wall, I turned into the door to the kitchen and cursed. It was not the kitchen. I stood in the entrance to an enormous open space with high, arched ceilings. It was ornate, but not like the council buildings of the village. The dark walls were wreathed in deep burgundy and velvet, and intricate stone constructs bore the flickering light of so many torches. A raised platform stood in the center of the back wall, holding a grouping of elaborate chairs, the largest of which was unquestionably meant to be the focus.

My mouth went dry. I was standing in the throne room.

My feet moved toward it automatically. I gave no mind to the warnings I'd received from the others. They'd not mentioned it specifically, but of all the things I'd been advised against, I was pretty sure what I was doing would fall into the not-a-good-idea category. It was one more place in the castle I shouldn't have been exploring alone, one more thing that wasn't safe for me until I'd recovered.

A shiver crawled over my skin as I reached out to touch the design along the crest of the throne. Again, I remembered the day I'd woken from the battle. I'd been more than a little slow to understand. I'd spent weeks reading my mother's diary, her words spelling the whole thing out, but it hadn't crossed my mind once that I was in line for the throne, as she had been.

But I'd seen the gathering outside my window. Chevelle had handed me my sword, and I'd raised it overhead to claim my place as Lord of the North.

I smirked. That hadn't lasted long. Since I couldn't remember my previous life and didn't have the slightest idea how to rule, I'd been kept from public view, "just until we straighten things out."

I hadn't caught up with the details, but apparently no one had truly ruled since the massacre my mother had started so long ago. Since there wasn't exactly a set routine, the seven elves who had returned me were calling themselves my guard and had taken to setting things in order—privately, so no one could guess I was out of sorts. But it was my throne. I felt myself smiling as I rolled the idea around in my mind.

"Looks like the cat finally got her canary," Steed teased from the doorway. I reined in my grin as a hawk swooped through the door, flapping a wing inches from Steed's shoulder then drifting to land on the carved pedestal beside the throne. It shook out its feathers, their snap reverberating softly through the hall. I thought I remembered the bird from some of the memories that weren't quite mine—it must have been a pet of sorts. But it couldn't have been the same hawk. I'd surely been gone too long for that.

Steed was still looking at me, waiting for a reply while I was lost in thought. "Steed," I gushed, and he looked pleased. I choked back the enthusiasm, clearing my throat. "You and Anvil have been gone. I thought the pair of you had left."

He leaned a hip against a side table, crossing his arms in front of his chest. "Just checking on some things nearby. But we will be going soon."

Despite my best efforts, I knew disappointment was plain on my face. I flopped down on the chair, forgetting it was a throne.

Steed stepped forward, coming close enough to brush my cheek with a knuckle. "Frey, someone has to get the rest of your magic."

My stomach twisted at his words. They would hunt down the other council members, the ones who had bound me. They would have to kill them to release the hold on me, but it wasn't just that. I couldn't bear to see our group of eight separated. "I don't want you to go," I confessed, and for some reason that made him smile.

"What would you have us do, Frey?" Chevelle's voice from the doorway made me jump. I became intensely aware of the intimate distance between Steed and me. I straightened.

I'd assumed the question had been rhetorical, but Chevelle waited for my reply. I didn't know if it was because of who I'd been before or who I was supposed to be now, but I certainly didn't feel like I had any authority. Nor did I feel like that other Frey, adored and spoiled, second to the throne. But the idea only made me realize where I was sitting and what my chair symbolized.

I huffed out a frustrated breath, fighting the urge to argue. I wanted the bindings released, needing my magic and my memories, but I couldn't stomach the idea of staying there if they left. "Why can't we all go?"

Chevelle nearly rolled his eyes but caught himself. We'd had that conversation more than once. "Frey, we just got you back here. We can't leave. The North will be back in chaos in a short time. We've just given people hope."

I laughed at the idea that they had hope because of me then shook my head. Steed and Chevelle gave me a look that said they thought I could crack at any moment. It wasn't a look that I could get used to, though I'd seen it regularly enough. I ignored them, thinking of a way to leave the castle without giving the kingdom doubts about their leader, without revealing my condition.

Suddenly, something occurred to me. Steed's comment about cats and canaries replayed in my mind. I sat back in the chair and closed my eyes, falling into the mind of the hawk resting beside me. It was the one magic the binding had never taken from me, the one talent that made me unique. I flew from the castle and over the mountain, searching for what I needed.

I was aware of Chevelle arguing with Steed. "Why do you insist on making this more complicated?"

"She's not as weak as you think."

"You know the bindings are dangerous. And you've seen what the stress can do to her."

"She's safer with us."

"Is she?" Chevelle asked icily.

"They won't hurt her."

"You know, I can still hear you," I said, a moment before my eyes flickered open.

I could tell by their expressions that they did not know. I stood and walked down the steps in front of the throne. "It doesn't matter now," I said. "I've taken care of it."

As I walked from the room, Chevelle's expression turned, his fingers curling into the palm of his hand. I picked up my pace.

Eventually, I found one of the servants to guide me to my room. I was fairly certain her name was Ena, though I couldn't be positive because she looked peculiarly similar to another of the servants, whose name I couldn't remember at all. They both had long, dark hair woven into intricate braids that accentuated sharp features, but one of them was definitely taller.

There'd been no shortage of servants moving about the castle during the weeks since I'd woken, but I hadn't tried to remember them, not because I wasn't interested, but because of the way their gazes dropped or they found a new task just as I took note of their presence. It seemed awkward. But it wasn't as if they didn't know me, even if I couldn't remember them.

"The staff is in on the secret, Freya. It's not a formal thing. None of the details were laid out for them, but they would have seen clearly enough. Anyone in the castle would have known something was wrong," Ruby had explained, flipping her scarlet curls. "Not to worry. They've proven their loyalty. They waited here, stayed in this empty castle, anticipating their lord's return." Her eyes had leveled on mine. "It's what they wanted." And then she'd lit up the practice room with fire and demanded that I fight my way through it.

I bit down hard against a rush of irritation when I realized that Ena had stopped outside my door, but I'd kept walking at least a half dozen more steps before noticing. It baffled me that I still did not have any idea where my room was. It was beginning to get under my skin, and it didn't help that the lost feeling wasn't any better inside the room. Sure, I could tell it was the room I'd been sleeping in, but it didn't feel like mine— not that the tree I'd lived in back in the village would anymore, either. That life felt so far away that I couldn't even grasp it.

I sighed. How bizarre it was that sleeping outside with a group of strangers had begun to feel like home.

I ran a fingertip across the table by the door. It was near bare, holding only a few books of no real interest, an empty marble dish, and a jeweled pin in a style I couldn't imagine ever liking. The whole room felt impersonal. I wondered if someone had removed my things, maybe in the years I was absent, or perhaps if it was all I'd ever had. I glanced around the room and focused on the nightstand, which held no more than an assortment of blades and a boot clip. My stomach tightened, and I walked past the sheer silks draping the wide, pillow-covered bed, heading to the window to look out over the mountain.

The sky was a clear, sharp blue that melted into the mists hovering over the land below. The view was comforting, more so than anything else in the castle, but still, it was only a moment before my thoughts turned once more to Chevelle. It was obvious he was avoiding me, keeping a formal distance, but I didn't know how to change that. I'd tried, a few days after it became apparent what he was doing, but that had ended in disaster.

We'd been alone in the practice rooms, trying to develop my control. I had decided that I could break his resolve, but I had been concentrating so hard on my seductive face and the look in my wanting eyes that I'd forgotten to pay attention to my cursed feet. I'd been moving in for the kill when I tripped, falling flat on my face. He turned away when I looked up, and I was sure I saw him smile. A flush tore back into my cheeks at the memory of him fighting that smile, that laugh, and I flopped on the bed, buried my face in the pillows, and prayed for sleep to come quickly.

I VOWED to myself that I would keep my dignity, but that was forgotten early the next morning, when Ruby woke me for training. I found myself groaning and complaining as she dragged me to the practice rooms to work with fire. She'd given me the it's-for-your-own-protection speech again, and I had to choke down further comment while she threw bits of flame toward me.

We hadn't been at it long when the cats showed up.

"Frey, Chevelle would like a word with you," Anvil spoke in the tone of official business from the doorway of the massive, open room. Still, I thought I saw a smile tease the corner of his mouth.

"What is it?" I asked, dropping my defenses to stare at my most solidly built guard.

"Best you come," was his only answer.

I took a deep breath as I followed him out with Ruby and Grey behind me. We went through the lower levels of the castle, where the staff carried on with their daily work, their heads down and their attention glued to their tasks. Anvil led the way as we wordlessly passed a group of sentries doing repairs to a block wall and another on patrol. Near the entrance to the castle, we found Chevelle, Steed, Rhys, and Rider.

Chevelle did not look happy. "Can you please explain to me why there is a pride of wild cats waiting for entrance to the castle, Frey?"

There should have been more than a simple clowder. I'd found as many mountain lions as I could and lured them to the castle. I tried to see past Chevelle then subtly raised to my toes to see over his shoulder. I barely caught a glimpse of golden fur glistening over a sleek, muscular body before Chevelle stepped forward, blocking my view.

It was more than evident that he wanted to put a strong hand on my shoulder to flatten my feet and keep me still. Instead, he peered into my eyes in an apparent attempt to force the answer from me with sheer will.

I sighed. "The cats will watch the castle for us." *Obviously.*

Ruby cracked a laugh, and everyone spun to glare at her. "She's right," she said, gesturing toward the cats. "I mean, who's going to doubt her powers now?"

They didn't exactly argue, but a silent chain of smirks and glares passed through the group. After several agonizing minutes, they apparently decided Ruby was right that the cats would leave no doubt as to my power. Chevelle shook his head and dismissed us to go back to training.

As Ruby and I left, Steed remarked in a low aside, "The wolves are going to love this."

I felt a pang of regret—I hadn't considered that. I'd barely seen the wolves since we'd arrived. I assumed they were outside, guarding us as usual.

Ruby elbowed me as we walked side by side through the corridor. I smiled back at her. We were all going together.

2

WITHIN A DAY, WE GATHERED, READY TO LEAVE THE CASTLE. THE plan was to depart before dawn, drawing as little attention as possible. I'd made arrangements with Dree from the kitchen staff to feed the cats, and I fervently hoped none of them would attack the servants. *Except maybe that big one who offered to give me a bath*, I thought, the shiver of revulsion making me twitch.

Everyone was staring at me. I managed a timid smile and got the collective look that said they were waiting for me to lose it.

But I didn't care. Shrugging it off, I mounted my horse, so glad to finally be doing something. All we needed was to find one more council member, and I would be that much closer to having my mind back. I wouldn't have to worry about how the bindings stole my memories and my magic, or when they became overtaxed, even affecting my ability to simply stay upright.

That was the worst part. The harder I tried and the closer I came to breaking free, the tighter they bound me, bringing me to my knees—or worse. At times, I had been lost to darkness for I didn't know how long and had woken exhausted from a dream-filled sleep. I had heard whispers since our return, and I understood that the others had not been merely concerned for the amount of time I had spent lost to that darkness, but also because of the violence with which it took me.

I kicked the horse up, leading the others through the gates.

Chevelle was beside me in a moment, his expression amused.

"What?" I asked defensively.

He merely tilted his head toward the others, who were heading in the opposite direction. *So much for doing this with dignity,* I thought, turning to follow them.

We made our way down the mountain on a path that exited the castle from behind. I wondered briefly if we would wind around to where we had come from weeks before, or if we would be headed somewhere new. But it was all so new to me. Such a short time ago, the village had been all I'd known, the whole of my world. None of the land was familiar to me. Everything and everyone were just shadows of memory.

I scanned the landscape, trying to distract myself from the journey I'd been so adamant about taking. I couldn't see much in the dimness, but the haze eventually thinned, and light from the rising sun started to peek through, allowing me a better view of the area. I spotted a pen of what looked to be boar in the distance. Ruby had explained to me how the elves there herded the animals and kept them until they were needed. The game on the mountain's peak was too sparse to keep up with the population, and there was very limited foliage. I didn't see anything I would have called vegetation amongst the rocks, but she assured me it was there, and despite an apparent aversion to growing, the castle held at least two gardens that I knew of.

I'd read about the feasts in my mother's diary, and I knew it must have taken a fair number of animals to sustain the castle's needs. There would be more pens and more corralled beasts, and it reminded me of an idea I'd had before the battle: *I could keep some animals handy for whenever I needed them, in case we get attacked...*

I shuddered at the thought. We weren't about to get attacked—we were on our way to *find* a fight. I suddenly wondered why I hadn't waited until I had trained more. *Why hadn't I kept my big mouth shut?*

"Cold?" Steed asked.

"Um, no. I'm fine." The conversation I'd been missing was about the horses, and I jumped in, trying to cover my lapse. "What's your horse's name?" I asked Steed.

His eyes met mine, and in a casual tone he answered, "I've named her Elfreda."

Heat flooded my cheeks, and he grinned. The jangle of Ruby's bracelets behind me gave me no doubt that she was the one who'd told him I'd named my horse Steed, which I probably would have thought twice about if I'd known how things were going to turn out. I shot her a glare, and Steed leaned forward, patting his horse's neck to cover his laugh.

The way was rough, and I found that I liked riding up the mountain better than down. Maybe the old Frey was a good rider, or maybe it was only my nerves, but leaning back all day to avoid being tossed over the horse's head wasn't exactly enjoyable. Plus, we had not, as far as I could tell, swung back around toward the south side of the mountain. The stones were darker on the north side, less traveled, and kind of eerie. When we finally stopped for the evening, I slid from the horse and walked through the jagged rocks surrounding the trail while I waited for dinner and a fire.

The others were in an official-sounding conversation that

I clearly wasn't expected to be a part of, so after a while, I busied myself by investigating what Ruby had packed for me. When I opened the first bag, my stomach knotted—it was full of weapons. I told myself they were for training, not for what lay at the end of our journey, and pulled out two knives. The blades were shiny and disturbingly sharp. I gingerly slid them back into the bag and took out a less offensive looking weapon, two sticks connected end to end by a thin metal chain.

It looked fairly harmless so, satisfied with my find, I stood to try it out. I had a hand on each end and gave them a pull, as if I were testing the chain. I had no idea what I was doing but figured it looked right. The contraption seemed to be pretty sturdy, but I couldn't decide how to use it in both hands, so I went with one. I'd seen Grey spin a staff and I thought I would try that method, holding the end of one stick in my right hand and swinging it carefully in a circle. It worked out nicely, so I swung it in a figure eight that wrapped around my sides. I found it went better with momentum, so I sped up a bit.

I really liked it. I got brave and tried out some new moves.

That was when the free end cracked the bridge of my nose.

Eyes watering, I risked a glance at the group to see if they had noticed.

They had. To their credit, they were trying to hold back their laughter, but it didn't matter. I had to save the embarrassment for later. My face hurt too badly to think of much else.

Pressing the base of my palm between my eyes, I sat blindly on one of the rocks behind me. I scowled beneath my forearm when I heard a low chuckle, sure it was Steed. Our journey had barely begun, and I'd already proven I was in over my head, which stung worse than the bridge of my nose.

I COULDN'T REMEMBER FALLING asleep, but I knew I was dreaming because I was the other Elfreda again. I was younger and braver, and though I couldn't lose the confusion even when dreaming, I was in control.

We were outside, but the ground was rocky, and the trees were low and spiky. We hid as we waited, pleased with ourselves as we watched our plan play out perfectly. Aunt Fannie had found our decoy. She was younger too, but old me still disliked her.

She spotted the scroll and checked to see that she wasn't being followed. She'd not seen us. Her eyes widened at the words on the page before she softly whispered them aloud. Beside me came a stifled chuckle as Chevelle worked his magic, burning lines into her palms. She dropped her prize then froze as she took in the image on her skin. It was false map that would lead her in circles for days, giving us time.

I JERKED AWAY from Ruby's touch as she tried to wake me. It was dawn. I was covered in sweat and muddled, confused. All I could see was that image burned into Fannie's skin.

Had it been a dream? It had to be that I had taken the real memories of the map I had found, which had led me north—led me to the castle—and combined them into a dream. Nothing else made sense. It could not have been memory.

But Chevelle had been with me as we tricked Fannie. I couldn't believe it. It must have been a dream because I could not fathom why he would have deceived me in the same way. I shook my head, hastily grabbing my things as the others waited.

The images nagged at me all day. They would not be

quieted even as we rode down the mountain, farther and farther from the castle.

I tried to remember the words that had called up the magic to draw the lines on my flesh. I was almost certain of them—it had been such a shock at the time to find a map burnt into my skin. When I couldn't resist any longer, I held back from the group as we rode and whispered the spell: "Fellon. Strago. Dreg."

Nothing happened.

Maybe I'd used the wrong words. But no, I was sure. Maybe it was a spell that only worked once. But I'd never heard of that, either, not that I knew that much about spells.

Spells had been forbidden in the village, to be used only by Council. They were certainly not for the likes of me.

Maybe I was already there, so there was no reason for the map to appear burned into my palms. However, the lines had disappeared before—I'd been riding into the village where we had met Ruby.

My mind returned over and over to that point and to the idea that it could be a memory, not a dream. But my hands were clean, and I held fast to the one shred of evidence I could muster: no one had the power to heal.

We were stopping before I realized it was evening. I was exhausted from worry.

Ruby must have been able to tell something was wrong. "Ooh, you should have put some snow on that." She giggled, pointing to my black eyes from the previous day's self-taught sticks-on-a-chain lesson.

I managed to glare at her, but it hurt more than it was worth.

We sat as Chevelle lit a fire, and I tried not to eye him suspiciously. I'd once marveled at how good he was with a flame and thought that maybe he had some sort of reversible burning power. *Now you're just making things up*, I chided myself. I considered the incident at the creek again, when the map had first appeared on my palms. He'd been so sincere later, when he'd said he had to take me north—once I saw the map, I was compelled to follow it. He regretted that he hadn't been paying closer attention. *I'm sorry, Freya. I let my guard down.*

He couldn't have burned the map into my palms. He'd said he'd been distracted. He'd had his own agenda—I'd watched him the night before as he snuck into a strange village and through a window for a secret meeting.

I froze as I made the connection. "What about Junnie?"

Ruby shot a quick glance at Chevelle, but his eyes didn't stray from the fire. She looked away, busying herself by rummaging in her pack as he answered, "What *about* Junnie?"

"I saw her when we were being attacked." I swallowed hard at the memory, forcing myself to stay on track and not to think of the day I'd nearly lost myself to the bonds in my mind.

Chevelle did look at me then, but I had my own answer about Junnie. My voice was weak as I talked myself through it. "She's a member of Council. She received the calling just before I left the village."

He let me digest that, but I was sure the fog in my brain and the breaks in my memory were keeping me from being able to make sense of it.

For all of those years, Junnie had been my only friend in the village, but it turned out that she hadn't been merely a friend at all. As my mother's aunt, she was my family. I'd read in my mother's diary how Junnie had come to see her, to warn her. I replayed my memories of the days in Junnie's study, of her lessons. She'd been kind to me. There was no question about that. Even though she would never have let on that she was any more than my mentor, it certainly wasn't the only thing she'd kept from me. She might have helped me with my studies, but she'd never truly taught me about magic.

I hadn't been sure then that I could even do magic. I had fire, though, and one morning, Chevelle had shown me how to control the tiny flame I'd been using since I'd arrived at the village.

"Frey?"

Ruby's voice pulled me from the spiraling thoughts. I looked up at her, away from the warmth and flicker of the camp's fire. I could feel the tension in my face.

The pity in her eyes made it easy to believe that our group was as important to her as it had become to me. It was all either of us had. She was alone but for a half brother and a missing father, and my only family were my two aunts, although I couldn't be sure whether I could count either. Thoughts of Fannie replaced my stress over Junnie.

And then something gnawed at the edge of my memories, a forgotten dream of Aunt Fannie, glorious in her anger—

"Frey." Ruby's voice was harsher than before. "It will be dark soon. We should continue your training." I had the feeling she was trying to distract me. Someone always interfered when they saw the strained look on my face as I fought with the bonds and the memories. A chill wind cut across my skin.

Ruby choked out a laugh as she scrutinized my bruised face. I narrowed my eyes at her when she said, "I'm guessing you don't want to try weapons today."

3

TRAINING WAS AS BRUTAL AS ALWAYS, BUT I HAD A HARDER TIME than usual because I couldn't stop my mind from returning to Junnie and Fannie. I wished there was a way to retrieve my memories and stop the ridiculous eddy of dreams and recollections. I cringed as I realized the most likely way was the one we were taking: hunting down and destroying those who'd bound me.

Instantly, worry set in. There was no guarantee it would work and no guarantee that no one would be hurt. It was why they'd had to be so careful with me before and so valiant in their watch against Council. I was determined to keep working and not to think of the flames.

But I did have that memory of the fire that had taken my mother, and it made me reconsider what I'd read in her diary. I hadn't wanted to finish it after the revelation that my father had been human, the description of my mother's own father and his wicked plans, and her depiction of the madness that led her to destroy the North.

I glanced around the camp as I sat alone with Ruby beside

me, her legs curled beneath her, giving her a bit of height. The others spoke in hushed tones across from us. It didn't make sense that they'd survived. The reports I'd seen of the Northern clans had claimed extinction.

"Ruby?"

She smiled as she answered, always anticipating something entertaining. "Hmm?"

It was hard to find the words. "What happened when my mother…"

Her brow tightened as I trailed off. "We don't have to talk about this now, Frey."

"I want to know," I said, but it didn't sound convincing.

She shook her head, light glinting in her emerald eyes. "You *think* you do."

"Would you be happier if you never knew…" I lost my words, unable to finish or to point out that she'd poisoned her own mother and who-knew-how-many others by accident.

Her reply was cool. "Wouldn't I?"

I sighed, scooping up a rock only to toss it aside. Ruby was probably right, but not knowing was torturous. "But she couldn't have… I mean, you are from the North, as are Steed and Chevelle." As I waved toward them for emphasis, I noticed Chevelle watching me. Staring at me. My throat went thick. My mother had killed his clan. "She didn't kill them all?"

Ruby's face flashed with sympathy and then irritation before reaching a third emotion that I couldn't quite make out. "No, Frey," she said, "but most remained scattered until things settled a bit."

I let out a deep breath, gaining at least some relief.

She eyed me suspiciously. "Frey…"

Uh-oh.

"What made you think she'd killed them all?"

I bit my lip, forcing my gaze to stay on hers. "Um, I read it?"

Her eyes narrowed. "That wasn't in the diary."

I hesitated, not wanting to admit anything about my research project but unable to skirt the truth. My thumb slid over the sharp edge of another rock. "It was in some papers from the village."

Her eyes flicked to Chevelle then back to me. He was still watching, but his face had gone hard.

Ruby's words were very nearly an accusation. "I thought you burned those."

"The ones from Council, yes. These were from the library." I glanced from Ruby to Chevelle, seeing that it troubled them but unsure why. Suddenly, my brain caught up, and I turned back to Ruby. "Wait, *you* read the diary?" It came out a little sharper than I'd intended.

She almost blanched. Instead, she answered matter-of-factly, "It was of interest to me."

Before I had time to respond, Chevelle was beside us. I was startled, and then I flushed because it was the closest he'd been since my failed seduction, and I couldn't seem to rein in even my minor reactions.

He seemed oblivious. "That wasn't in the documents you found at the library."

I flushed anew. He *had* seen the documents at the library and knew I had been researching him.

He waited for my answer.

"Um, I found these before."

"In the library?" He was still serious.

"Yeah." And then I remembered, pointing vaguely upward despite the fact that we were currently not in the village or the library. "Actually, they fell from a higher level."

They were staring at me as though I'd missed something

obvious, something they didn't like. Ruby interjected, "Frey, are you sure you didn't pull them to you with magic?"

"I don't think so," I said, leaving the "how would I know?" implied.

They stared at me.

"What?"

Chevelle was close and in careful mode, the one they used to protect my delicate brain. I nearly snickered at the thought but didn't—it clearly wasn't the time for that. "Were there any other documents, papers, *anything*, that you found?"

The way he said "found" confused me. "I don't know."

He waited while I reconsidered.

"There were those, and the ones in the library the day you helped me study…" He hadn't been helping me study, he'd been watching me. I huffed out a breath. "And then the ones in the council library."

"Nothing else?"

"Only the scroll."

They both glanced away, almost flinching, before Chevelle turned his focus back to me. "Are you sure?"

"Yes, but it didn't matter. They were all messed up, anyway."

His fingers tightened against the hilt of the sword at his hip. "What do you mean, 'messed up'?"

"They were all out of order, just loose pages." His eyes narrowed, and I couldn't stop myself from talking. "The stuff about the Northern clans was mixed in with stuff about Fannie and you—"

I stopped suddenly when it looked as though he might have paled. I couldn't be sure because before I could get a good look, he was gone. I watched after him for a moment then turned to Ruby, who was expressionless.

"What is it, Ruby?" I whispered.

She composed a polite smile. "Nothing, dear. You should get some sleep."

I glared at her, not for the first time, and received no response. They weren't going to tell me anything. They were too worried about my fragile brain.

I flipped a blanket out a few feet from the fire and flopped down onto the hard earth, frustrated and annoyed. I wondered if I could get someone else to tell me, maybe Steed. It could be worth a try, but I didn't know about the others. I liked Grey very much, though I had my suspicions he hung around more for Ruby than anything else. Rhys and Rider were always on the periphery, watching and guarding. That only left Anvil.

I glanced in his direction, finding only the vague outline of his form among the mist. There was definitely something about Anvil—I'd been drawn to him since the first time we'd met, wanting to be his friend. It didn't seem right, though. He was massive, not to mention the fact that he could shoot lightning from his hands, and he should have been frightening. The feelings I had toward him, that inexplicable pull, didn't match my dreams of his tongue wagging then being burned and torn away.

I groaned, rolling over as I tried to remove the image from my mind. There had to be another way. Maybe there was more in the diary. I should have kept reading it, but I hadn't wanted anything else to do with it once I'd found out. I wondered where it was. I couldn't remember seeing it after I woke. The last time had been the night Chevelle had tossed it aside, when he'd held me as I wept. There were so many images I had to banish from my mind.

And then inspiration hit. Surely, we were still close enough…

I closed my eyes and concentrated until I found what I

needed. My new talent seemed better all the time. I was in the mind of one of the mountain lions I'd left in the castle, seeing through his eyes. His vision was clearer, but it was harder to stay focused than with the horses.

He didn't cooperate as well as I would have liked, but I was able to get him to move from his comfortable spot. I couldn't discern exactly where that spot was, but when I tried to look around, the cat became distracted by the sight of blood, and I had to focus harder to keep him moving. I really hoped that was whatever Dree was feeding them and not Dree herself.

The cat had been lounging high on a ledge, possibly in the throne room. I was still confused by the layout of the castle and not sure how to get the cat where I wanted, but I could embody its mind and thought I knew where we needed to search: Ruby's room.

As we wandered through the corridors, my head began to ache. The halls of the faraway castle were unusually empty, and I didn't know if that had anything to do with the presence of the cats. I tried several rooms, but most that were open held nothing of interest.

I was wondering how I would ever find Ruby's room and the diary when I came to a set of double doors I'd never seen before. They looked more ornate than the others, with intricate iron details and arched stonework around the frame, which showed promise, proof of their importance. With some effort, I reached a heavy paw up to pull the lever that released the latch. The cat was bigger than I'd realized, and his weighty body pushed the door right open.

He slinked forward toward the sheer-curtained bed, and I let him, looking around as we went. It seemed easier to ride along than to constantly try to control his movement, but I couldn't decide if that was due to the distance or the animal.

He pounced on the curtains, pulling them loose, and lazily plopped down on the end of the bed to survey the room.

I wasn't sure how to know when I'd found Ruby's bedroom, let alone where to look for the diary, but it was definitely a woman's room. There were rich fabrics everywhere and dresses draped over the wardrobe door, but they were dusty. Upon closer inspection, I realized it couldn't have been Ruby's room—it obviously hadn't been used for what seemed to be an exceptionally long time. I wondered why the servants hadn't cleaned it.

An annoyed rumble rolled from the cat as I tried to move off the bed to get a better look at the items on the vanity. We didn't budge. My head was throbbing, but I pushed harder. He refused to behave as I wanted, and I wondered if the cat's resistance to my direction was why so many fewer than I'd planned had shown up at the castle.

Suddenly, his muscles tensed, and he turned his head at some commotion nearing the door. He moved too quickly, and I struggled to concentrate on making out the shouts over approaching footfalls.

"The seal has been broken... Miss Vita's room... No, no, by one of the cats..."

I didn't know whether it was the pain in my head or recognition of the name that brought me back, but I was gone from the castle in a heartbeat, the link broken. I sat up on my blankets, rubbing my temples as I attempted to focus on what I'd heard.

Vita was my mother's mother, according to the diary. She'd died from grief, it had said. My mother had tried to see her and her room later, but it was sealed, kept from her by her father.

Ruby was watching me. "Headache?"

Having an audience had become unsurprising. I opened

my mouth to speak but was too exhausted. Instead, I only shook my head and lay back down. It was nearly impossible to examine the memories between the exhaustion and pain, so I tried to not think as I drifted off to sleep.

I felt better when I woke but was still foggier than usual. It was late morning when I remembered I was mad at Ruby for keeping something from me. I shot a glare in her direction, finding only her back as she rode. I focused on the drape of her cloak and her bright-red curls knotted into a scarf.

Steed noticed my scowl. "Don't be sore with Ruby."

I raised an eyebrow at him, drawing my own cloak tighter around me as the horses stepped over loose stone.

"She had her reasons for the invasion. She's very interested in your… lineage."

I realized he was talking about her having read my mother's diary, and my irritation flared. I had forgotten that part.

Steed had stopped talking, so I composed my face and waited for him to continue, trying to appear patient. He smiled at my attempt, and we fell back from the others.

"You know some of her story, that she's a half-breed," he said.

Patience was a hard thing.

He could tell I was struggling and winked. "I should start from the beginning. It will be a long ride, after all." His grin died as he began what I knew would be a somber story. "My mother and father had a happy life. Their differences fit nicely together, and their bonds were strong. But the horses couldn't thrive on the mountains that my mother loved, and my father traveled often to find new blood to bring in for the line. He was gone sometimes for months at a time, as was I, once I began to learn the trade." His hand fell automatically to the shoulder of the beast beneath him, and he ran his fingers over the smooth dark hair. "Which is why we were both absent during the incident in which she lost her life."

I stifled a groan, sure the "incident" he referred to was the massacre single-handedly caused by my mother.

"We returned separately, as I was detained in another matter, so I was not there when he received the news."

I realized I was holding my breath and focused on matching it to the rhythm of the hoofbeats. I wondered if Steed's father had the same short dark hair and easy smile, if he had the same way with the horses.

"When I finally saw him, he was beyond distraught. He was not himself. I was fearful for him, but I too was in mourning. Likewise, I had my own duties to fulfill. So I was gone again when the second tragedy befell him."

Ruby's mother.

"The fey woman found him in such a condition that it was effortless to sway him with enchantments. All this you know. What Ruby has left out is the root of the issue. Yes, you are similar in that you are both from unmatched parents."

I very nearly laughed at his term.

"But the real reason she was interested in your mother's diary was because… Well, you were what sparked the idea in her own mother's twisted mind."

I was lost, and he could tell.

"You see, Frey, your mother was bred"—he paused, pursing his lips as if changing his mind—"*created* for uniqueness. But you? You were born with it."

I couldn't think of my own mother or of myself, labeled a crossbreed, so instead I thought of Ruby. *Uniqueness.* "Well, she got it, didn't she?" I knew we were both thinking of her venom when we looked at her.

29

She turned back with a half smile and shot us a wink. I could see why Steed had helped her, despite everything. After all that her mother had done to destroy his family, it almost gave me hope. It seemed that the group had forgiven me for my mother's actions as well.

I wondered how clearly those actions might have been detailed in the diary. "I wish I'd finished reading it."

"Why don't you?"

"I don't know where it is."

"I'm sure Ruby has it. She carries everything she values with her."

The possibility almost had me clicking my heels to catch her, but she was riding near Chevelle. He tended to get annoyed at this sort of thing, and I still had an odd feeling about him, given the dream, the memory, and the strange lines that had curved over my palms. I tried to shake it off but stayed back with Steed.

I had a lot to avoid thinking about as we rode, so I bantered with him like we had when we first met. It was nice to be out of the castle, to breathe the cool mountain air, to be away from so many shifting eyes, and to have a purpose, even if I had to keep from questioning what our purpose was so that I didn't make myself sick with worry. When Steed and I talked, laughter came easily, and soon, the group's pace slowed as everyone joined in the conversation.

The casual mood continued throughout the day, and all seemed in good spirits when we stopped earlier than usual for the evening. I groaned when Ruby suggested training before dinner, so Chevelle offered to spar with me. He knew it was something I enjoyed—it was the only training that was tolerable, mostly because I didn't get hurt, though it also wasn't as tiring as practicing with Ruby. Nothing about it taxed those bindings in my mind and on my powers. Everyone gathered around to watch as Chevelle and I clashed swords, a rhythmic clinking the only sound besides the occasional comment or murmur of approval from the makeshift audience.

As it often did when I trained with Chevelle, time slipped by faster than I'd realized. It was getting dark when he straightened and lowered his sword. I tried to wipe the grin off my face—I knew I was improving immensely. Someone lit a flame, and our audience moved to surround it. I started to follow, but Chevelle stood still for a moment, simply watching me. His eyes were bluer in the waning sun, and he must have forgotten to mask his features.

He didn't speak, and the pressure of silence built in me, bringing all sorts of things that I shouldn't say to the tip of my tongue. He made no move to ease the tension, and I panicked, fearing something as disastrous as my last attempt. I blew out a nervous breath, hurrying past him to join the others.

Apparently, the tension had been all mine. He didn't guard his countenance, even as I glanced at him frequently during dinner.

It seemed he was watching me, too, but I'd been known to imagine things of that sort. After all, I was the one staring at him. I forced my eyes down, picking at my food, and the process of eating became daunting. Time passed, but I could still feel his eyes on me, even if he wasn't looking.

Wind cut through the sparse narrow trees, and Ruby came to sit beside me, smiling mischievously as she offered a small metal cup. I peered inside, suspicious of what appeared to be water, and she laughed, bumping my shoulder. When I raised it to my lips, she slipped a parcel onto my lap. It was the diary.

I glanced at her, knowing I shouldn't have been surprised that she'd heard, and she wiggled her eyebrows as she rose to play in the fire. The flickering light threw shadows across the leather binding of the diary. It was heavy in my hand, and I was suddenly unsure. Maybe Ruby was right about being happier not knowing.

I ran my fingers over the cover, etched with Vita's initial. I remembered once thinking it had stood for Vattier. I'd been wrong about so many things. I tucked it into my bag. After the day we'd had, I didn't want to lose the good feelings just yet.

I should have known better.

4

I'd fallen asleep thinking only of the patterns of crossing swords, choosing to avoid thoughts of Chevelle, so I was surprised to dream of Fannie.

It was a familiar dream, but I couldn't be sure why. I was taking in the scene from above, my vision slightly off. I could see her there, wild and violent. She was destroying the village around her, uprooting trees, burning them to ash. And she was laughing. As I watched the devastation, I recognized the villagers as my own, but even in my dream, that was not the worrisome part. Nor was it the broken bodies, the demolished grounds. There was something else, something I couldn't quite grasp...

I awoke unsettled. Although Ruby and the others remained in the previous day's elevated mood, I couldn't shake the feeling. I glanced around as we mounted and started back on our path. We'd covered some distance, and the terrain had settled slightly. It wasn't as steep or rocky, so I was able to relax in the saddle more. My thoughts kept returning to Fannie and the dream.

I suddenly realized I knew something about her that I was sure hadn't been explained to me by the others. I might have dreamt it, or it might have been there, unnoticed until I'd focused on the memory of her.

What I knew was that Fannie had been skipped. As the oldest daughter, she had been in line for the throne before her sister. Their father had, at least for all public purposes, disowned her, instead choosing my mother as his heir, his second. The details weren't all there in my mind, but I remembered from reading my mother's diary that from an early age, Fannie had been shunned for her light features, a product of her mother's heritage, and her lack of the power and uniqueness that her sister apparently possessed. She held more light magic, also like her mother, and he had disdained light elves.

It was disconcerting when the memories returned. Most of them came to me in dreams, which was confusing—parts of my previous life seemed strange enough to be dreams, while my dreams so often felt real enough to be memories.

Chevelle had once told me that he thought the memories found their way back more easily in my sleep because they didn't have to fight as hard to be released from their bonds while my mind was resting and unable to resist. It had made sense then, but I wasn't sure they couldn't just slip through at any time. Maybe they were already there, and I simply hadn't sifted through them enough.

A shiver ran through me, though I was wrapped in a heavy cloak, and when a rock clattered down the path, I flinched. It was only knocked loose by a horse hoof, and I was growing more self-conscious about how jumpy I'd become. I adjusted my position in the saddle and glanced at the others, who seemed oblivious to my jitters. Maybe they were just getting used to it.

The dream still shook me, so I closed my eyes and drifted

to the one thing that gave me solace: the bird soaring over-head. I glided for a while in large, calming circles over our group and eventually scanned farther. I attempted to survey the path ahead, but I wasn't positive where we were going. My hope was that if I did a sweep of the land every morning, or maybe a few times a day, I would spot danger ahead of time.

Suddenly, I was back in my own head again, wondering what I'd gotten myself into with hunting Grand Council, scoping out the perimeter, and planning to capture animals for use in battle. Maybe I *was* nuts—maybe those looks I'd been getting were rooted in something real.

But in the back of my mind, I had to fight the thought that going mad wasn't as far-fetched as I might like to think. It had happened to my own mother, after all. I felt my face pinch and tried to smooth it before someone noticed.

I realized they were otherwise occupied when Grey began whistling a tune and asked Anvil to join in, provoking him about his inability to do so due to a damaged tongue. Anvil flung a metal stud from his vest at him in retaliation, and it must have been carrying electricity because the instant it hit Grey, he jerked, almost losing his seat. Steed laughed, and it wasn't long before a mêlée between the three ensued. I was beginning to enjoy the spectacle, though it looked painful. Before it escalated further, Chevelle called over his shoulder, "I can think of a better use of your energy, men." However, I thought I saw him smirk when, several minutes later, Steed and Grey were still twitching.

Out of nowhere, an image came to my mind. For no apparent reason, I remembered someone. There was a split second of astonishment before fear choked me.

It must have been audible because instantly, the others were surrounding me. "What?" someone said, but I wasn't sure who. My ears were ringing, but I couldn't bring myself to be irritated because I was overwhelmed with terror that was quickly turning into hatred.

I made an effort to focus when Chevelle was in front of me. I thought he'd grabbed me by the arms and pulled me from my horse, but I couldn't be certain because when I was finally able to bring myself back to the moment, he was all I could see. It was good he was close, because I was only capable of a whisper when I said, "Archer Lake."

An intake of breath swept through my audience, although I could only see Chevelle's face. It was a study in fury. The name meant something to him as well, but I couldn't tell if it was more than simple recognition. All I knew about Archer Lake was that he was a member of Grand Council, and I hated him.

Someone asked where Archer Lake was, and I forced the sick feeling down enough to explain. "It wasn't a vision," I said. "Just a memory." As if I had returned from nowhere, missing essential pieces. "I don't know how I know him." I'd no idea from when, though it had to be from my previous life, surely, and no idea why it had come back. "Only the image of his face." And the knowledge of his station. And the feeling that accompanied them.

"Does that happen often?" Grey asked, his brows knitted beneath short, shaggy bangs.

I shook my head. "No. Just today."

"There's more?" Chevelle said.

"I'm not sure. I remembered something new about Fannie this morning."

He blanched.

It seemed like less of a coincidence all of a sudden. The dream of Fannie that had bothered me so much was creeping into my thoughts again, along with the one before that included Chevelle. I looked down at my hands, at the ground, at anything but him.

After a few minutes, Ruby collected herself enough to keep me occupied, per usual. She offered me some powder for my headache—which I refused, having been subjected to her concoctions in the past—and fluttered around doing things. I didn't watch her too closely, partially because the flow of her clothes and swing of her bright-red curls made my head ache, but mostly because I was forcing myself not to hope—and at the same time, fear—that my memory was returning.

The group made like there was a good reason we'd stopped for so long in the middle of the day, busying themselves as well. Steed adjusted the packs on the horses, Grey sorted and cleaned weapons, and Anvil stood with his arms crossed over his broad chest, staring into the distance.

When we finally got back on the horses, they took it easy until early evening, when we stopped again to set camp. I was impressed that they managed to make creating a fire and situating themselves around it a seven-man task.

No one even mentioned training.

THE NEXT MORNING, I was groggy—they'd let me sleep in. Grey and Anvil looked itchy to get back on the trail, so I hurried to mount my horse, taking my cold breakfast with me. The extra time had allowed for better hunting, and our bags were packed with stores of food. I couldn't believe I'd slept through the smell of cooking meat. I remembered how I used to love elk, but it was everyone else's favorite as well, which made it hard to come by on the mountain.

I froze, the chunk of meat suddenly heavy in my unmoving hand. My love of elk was another new memory. I examined it, unsure whether to explain it to the group. It was nothing aside from a preference, so I decided to let it go. I could tell them if I remembered more. Chevelle watching me, so I kicked my horse up as if I'd only been daydreaming.

We rode at a more normal pace as the ground leveled off a bit where the mountain valleyed into a smaller ridge. The rocks were changing again, and I looked back toward the castle to see how far we'd come, but between the distance and fog, I couldn't see it. I wondered how the cats were doing. When they'd arrived, there had been more than one fight— they were extremely territorial, and I couldn't seem to convince them otherwise. They were complicated animals.

It made me curious about how other animals would react. I'd had pretty limited experience so far, but birds had proven very useful.

I recalled my plan and looked up, trying to find a vessel to scan the mountain again. There was a large red-tail, a nice one with good eyes. I briefly considered bringing it with us, in case I wasn't able to find one when the urge struck, but there seemed to be plenty available, so I took a brief survey of the land around us then let it be.

We continued that way for days, following the valley for more passable ground. Twice, I spotted the wolves. It made me feel more secure to know they were out there, but I still did a quick sweep from above at least three times a day. The feeling of foreboding grew worse the farther we traveled from the castle, and my paranoia increased as we closed in on our destination, wherever that was.

Then Ruby decided to start telling her fey stories, which, since I knew they were probably all true, only made things worse. I tried to ignore her by flying over the valley, gliding over a spectacular view. The gray rock was beginning to give way to vegetation, and deep-green trees had started to appear more and more frequently. I found myself counting them, marking their patches. *Dark green, dark green, dark green.*

"Does that not tire you?"

Where I might have jumped, surprise didn't have the expected reactions in the bird's body, but it pulled me back to myself. I opened my eyes to find Anvil riding beside me, watching.

I grinned at him automatically then remembered he'd asked a question. "Oh, um… I guess not, not really."

"That's good," he said, smiling, and I had to brace myself from reacting to the thought of his burning tongue. He was such a contradiction—part of me was so drawn to him, so trusting, while the other part reeled at the image in my dreams. I pushed the memory down, thinking instead of his talent and how it exhausted him of strength.

"The lightning tires you, huh?" I asked. Sometimes I thought I sounded like an idiot, mostly when I wanted to impress someone.

He didn't seem to notice, resting the heel of his hand on the pommel as he leaned forward. "Yes. But it's worth it, I think."

"How did you think to try?"

He laughed lightly. Apparently, I didn't get the joke.

I found myself wondering if I could do it and concentrated on my hands while we rode, willing electricity through them. Nothing happened. I didn't really expect it to, but then I saw Anvil's wide grin, and I grimaced at forgetting he was beside me. *Yep, usually just people I want to like me.*

But he did like me, and he was part of my guard. I lowered my voice. "Anvil?"

He shifted toward me, and I struggled to find the right way to ask. "What do you know about me?"

He stared at me while I waited for his answer. And then I

was thrown forward in the saddle as my horse came to a sudden stop. Chevelle's horse was inches in front of mine, blocking us.

"Frey, we've been neglecting your training," he said. "You should work with Anvil as you ride."

I tried to hide my reaction, but it was too late.

Anvil chuckled. "Don't think she relishes the lightning."

Chevelle was undeterred. "Grey, then."

Anvil smiled as he moved forward, and Grey fell in beside me, our horses joining the group's pace automatically as he began his version of training.

He was outfitted in dark leather, the unadorned sleeves cut widely to allow extra movement. "You know what I find helpful?"

"Being able to disappear and reappear?"

He laughed, and I softened. His eyes glinted as he grinned conspiratorially. "Distraction."

Our lesson continued throughout the day, and he was good at both the teaching and the distraction. I forgot most of what had been worrying me and concentrated on retaining Grey's tricks, practicing sleight of hand and diversions.

When we stopped to make camp, I stuck by Grey's side, content to keep on task with the nontaxing occupation. I didn't let myself be concerned about the diary or what waited inside. I didn't think about what the coming days might bring or where we were headed.

THE NEXT MORNING, I kept silent, hoping no one volunteered to teach me about a new weapon or something equally painful. But Ruby had taken to telling stories again, and no one mentioned my practice. I happily returned to the sky to hide from her terrible tales and the constant threat of practice and our eventual destination, but it was impossible to deny when I could see that we were traveling toward the territory of the light elves and the Council that wanted to destroy me.

The chill had fallen off, the haze clearer, and I examined our new surroundings from above. The sun warmed the colors of a patch of dormant weeds to almost golden, and the new color was such a pleasant change to the scenery that I kept looking, trying to pick out more.

What caught my eye next was so wrong that I couldn't quite process it. The pressure on my arm was the only indicator that I'd gasped.

I opened my eyes to find Ruby grasping my arm tightly and wearing a concerned expression. "What is it, Frey?"

"I don't know." I tried to sort my thoughts and place why what I'd seen seemed so important. I knew what was wrong with the picture. "Blond hair."

Their faces reflected mine, I was sure. It wasn't a dark elf.

"Was it a council member?" Ruby asked.

"I don't think so. She... well, she didn't look like it. And there was a man with her. He had a dark cloak with a hood."

"Where?" Chevelle snapped from my other side.

I hadn't noticed how close he was, and it took a moment to find the answer. "About two miles." As soon as I pointed out the direction, he was gone. I kicked up my horse, racing behind him and trying to keep up, but the others were faster, finding our target well ahead of me.

The seven of them were surrounding the strangers before I had a chance to see anything. I threw myself off my horse, leaving him where a couple of the other horses stood, and stumbled blindly toward the group. I pushed through where they had gathered, determined to not be kept out.

Chevelle's hand flew up to keep me back. I pressed, but his grip was strong on my shoulder, restraining me.

Rhys and Rider had beaten us all there. The plain black cloak was a pile on the ground in front of them. The man I had seen lay crumpled beneath it, motionless. His hair was dark, the carved leather of his bracer familiar somehow. My eyes fell on the girl, and I knew she was next.

I yelled, "Stop!"

And they did, if only to look at me.

My outburst couldn't have bought me more than a moment, but I wasn't able to capitalize on it because standing before me, on the other side of Chevelle and the outstretched arms of the tall, slender, silver-haired Rhys and Rider, was a sight my brain could not process.

But there it was, right in front of my wide eyes. The blond hair that I had seen from above framed a soft face, flushed cheeks, full lips, and round blue eyes filled with fear.

It can't be.

When the breeze caught her shoulder-length locks and flipped them back, it was just enough to reveal rounded ears.

I almost fainted. All that saved me was that in the split second before blackness hit, I saw a nod.

I knew what that nod meant. Chevelle, standing inches in front of me, was instructing the pair of elves before the human to end her life.

"No."

It came out with more desperation than I'd intended, but it caused them to hesitate. Chevelle looked at my face for a long moment, and I stared back at him with a wordless plea.

The seconds dragged on agonizingly. *I cannot let them do this.* Chevelle's face was hard as he finally turned from me and called it off. I wasn't sure why, but for an instant, I imagined it was because she was like me. I felt my cheeks color and looked down.

Then I slipped off the edge.

~

WHEN I CAME TO, I was convinced it had all been a dream. I almost laughed at the absurdity as I tried to sit up, holding my throbbing head. Ruby steadied me, purring something soothing as she handed me a drink of water. It helped. I opened my eyes, and she was right there, trying to hide the concern in her gaze. I wondered what was wrong with her then realized Chevelle was beside me as well. Though he was angled away, he turned to look at me when he noticed I was awake.

It irritated me that this fainting thing was becoming commonplace.

Ruby was unusually quiet and looked as though she might have been biting her tongue. I hoped I wasn't about to get dusted for some reason that I couldn't see. She'd used the powder on me more than once when I'd been bound, anytime my mind became overwhelmed.

I started to scan my surroundings, but Chevelle was blocking my view of the others, who seemed to be gathered several yards away, huddled around something. I leaned, straining to see past him, and he put a hand on my arm to steady me.

"Easy, Frey. You should rest more. Don't get too excited."

What?

"Just lie here for a while."

He wasn't trying to steady me. He was trying to restrain me. When my glare hit him, he reluctantly released my arm and straightened, allowing me to see.

At first, I was only numb. When I realized my jaw was hanging open, I snapped it closed and clenched it so tightly that I wondered if my teeth might shatter. I felt the heat in my cheeks. I wasn't getting enough air. But I couldn't release my jaw. I knew from much experience that I would regret what I was about to say, so instead, I just kept staring.

The others noticed I was awake as they talked with her and turned to gauge my reaction. I was surprised they were speaking with her as if she was... well, as if she was one of *us*. That idea turned my stomach, but they seemed genuinely interested in her. Especially Steed.

I felt the flush of my cheeks brighten when I gathered that he was *particularly* interested in her. He sat close, leaning in, as he often had in our private conversations, his voice too low to hear.

Ruby's face appeared unexpectedly in front of mine, her eyes wide, and I realized I was making a sound akin to a growl. I should have been attempting some kind of control, but I couldn't bring myself to care. An actual human was sitting there. It was just too much. It made everything too real.

Somehow, I'd still believed they didn't exist, though I'd read in my own mother's diary that I was half human. It was hard to deny when I was staring directly at what was indisputably one of them.

She was surrounded by the only thing I had, my friends, my family. A fire lit in my palms, and Ruby clasped her hands around my wrists. I knew she couldn't be burned because she was half fire fey, a hard lesson I had learned during training, but I wasn't sure it mattered. I had been teetering on a ledge for months. I couldn't even say where that ledge *was* anymore.

I was standing before I realized it. A brief flash of memory, too quick to act on, told me the mumbling chant coming from Chevelle was a problem.

Blackness hit.

~

IT WAS hard to say how long I'd been immobilized, but when I did finally regain control, I didn't want to move. My head throbbed, and my ears rang. I'd been down before. Chevelle wasn't causing the pain—that was me, fighting my own brain. I had to.

I knew Ruby was waiting beside me, anxious for me to respond, but I didn't. I couldn't manage any kind of composure.

Eventually, the ringing in my ears lessened enough that I could hear the girl's voice, which only agitated the turbulence in my mind more.

A human. I could not, would not, allow myself to be compared to *that*.

It was unreasonable, and I knew it, but the unbearable, unrelenting emotions tore their way through me anyway, tied to some darkness, some secret that I could not recall.

No one asked me to move or reminded me that we had a task to follow through with. No one did anything but entertain themselves with the cursed human.

Time passed. I had finally moved into a sitting position, facing away from all of them. A human in our camp felt too wrong—unacceptable—for a reason I couldn't quite identify, and it wasn't just that the others seemed to enjoy the oddity of her so much. True, Ruby and Chevelle kept their distance from her, but I had my suspicions that they were only staying near to keep me in line.

I stared down at my arms wrapped tightly around my knees, concentrating on picking at the dark fabric of my pants. When I heard a peculiar noise from her general direction, I wasn't able to stop myself from looking over my shoulder, a knee-jerk reaction. She was staring at me.

A very nasty thought crossed my mind, and I yelped when Ruby stomped my foot. Apparently, I'd said it aloud.

My toe throbbed, but Ruby was wrong if she thought I would be abashed. That girl had been eyeing me with pity. *Or like I'm mad.*

When the noise came again, I forced myself to ignore it, finding a spot farther away from the group. I mumbled under my breath that I should have let them lop her head off, and Ruby made a sharp sound, but I couldn't tell whether it was a laugh or a hiss.

The rest of the evening, spent on a rock well away from them, was hard, full of the bad feelings and foggy memories that haunted me. At nightfall, Chevelle came to get me. I didn't turn to him at first, imagining him smug—after all, he'd intended to be done with her right then and there. I'd been the one who stopped him. I hadn't wanted them to kill her.

That realization lessened my anger just enough to allow me to breathe. Irrational as it might have been, I was having serious trouble controlling my reaction.

Chevelle stepped beside me, standing to stare in the same direction I was. "We should continue tomorrow."

I glanced at him, unable to read the emotion on his face in the dying light. Honestly, I could really only be sure when he was angry, which he didn't appear to be. I nodded, and it seemed for a moment as if he might reach out to me to comfort me—or possibly to smack me for my tantrum—but he merely turned and walked away.

I sighed deeply before rising to follow him to the camp.

~

IT TURNED out I was able to cope with the human's presence by ignoring it completely. It might have been petty and childish, but it worked. It seemed that because I had spared her life before going into that lengthy sulk, she was now under the group's care, excluding, of course, Chevelle and Ruby, who were constantly throwing glances toward me... to check my stability, I presumed.

However, I had been a model of good behavior, except for one incident around the campfire. Once I was back with the group, it wasn't long before I saw the source of the peculiar noise. It was the yelp of a small, dark puppy the girl they'd been calling Molly kept tucked under her arm, hidden beneath her heavy shawl. When I'd proven capable of self-control, she'd given it more leeway, allowing it to romp and play for the delight of its new audience. *Her* new audience. At that moment, it inexplicably attacked, giving the girl a good, solid bite. Like I said, there was the one incident.

The girl had seemed baffled but had immediately forgiven the tiny black pup.

When we reached the base of the mountain, the overall discontent I'd been feeling since we'd left had spread through the group, building into stony silence. We were hunting down Grand Council. And we had a human... pet.

We made camp, and Ruby escorted the human from the group for privacy. It was Ruby's only real contact with her. I was glaring in their direction, wondering why she didn't just piddle on our blankets like the pup, when a catclaw seed smacked me in the back of the head. I whipped around but couldn't tell who had thrown it, so I gave up and sat on a low rock slab to wait for dinner.

That was when I realized they were talking about her. They were trying to be discreet, but I knew what they were saying. They were working out what to do with her, how to get rid of her. My chest tightened as I focused on the conversation.

"No," Chevelle said, his words making it entirely clear that he didn't trust Grey or Anvil with her. I couldn't understand why.

Grey shrugged. "What about the brothers?"

Chevelle's eyes shifted toward Rhys and Rider as he said, "They have refused."

Steed nodded once. "I'll do it."

I was talking before I could contain myself, the words sour. "Sure, you'll take her home." When they turned to stare at me, I realized I was furious. And that I was standing.

Chevelle's face was hard, and I had a flashback of the look he'd given me at Ruby's so long ago, when he thought I was jealous of her affection for Steed.

I swallowed hard, forcing myself to sit down, but it was too late. My outburst had cost me knowing their decision. I lowered my eyes to the ground as Ruby came back with the girl. I didn't know what was wrong with me, couldn't understand what it was about the idea of her that made me want to claw my chest out.

Am I truly going mad?

"Who's hunting tonight?" Ruby chirped, and the others pointed to anyone but her. They chattered as they prepared, as if nothing important was happening, as if it was just another day. For them, maybe it was. Maybe I was the only one who'd been blind to the existence of humans and who hadn't realized how much danger I was in.

After dinner, Ruby moved to sit with Grey and Anvil, telling more stories of the fey. I faded in and out of her tale of Violet Moon. "She came from the South," Ruby said, "farther than any area of record, and she possessed a wicked knowledge of the changelings."

Any chill faded, and I knew the flame twisted within the confines of the circle at Ruby's command. She would make it dance along with her words, make it flare and spark. "They say she was bored with her native land and traveled North, looking for those who would not know her disguises and deceits."

My head lay cradled in darkness, where my arms made a bridge across drawn-in knees, as Ruby began regaling us with Violet's seduction of a young fire fey, complete with plenty of unnecessary details of his physique, when Steed said my name. I looked up, across the fire to him, and I almost choked.

He hadn't exactly said my name. He'd used my nickname— well, my old nickname—on *her*. He'd called her Sunshine.

My face burned. Steed didn't notice my glare because he was still talking to her, laughing. He reached up to tuck her hair behind her ear, and I heard a loud pop, or maybe felt it. I was off balance for a moment before I realized it was fire.

I gasped, looking around to see if any of them noticed.

Everyone had, not that I could blame them. I had pushed fireballs out of my squeezed fists so hard it had actually been audible.

They stood motionless, staring at me until finally Ruby asked, "Frey, are you all right?"

I took stock. "Yeah." *What just happened?*

She took a tentative step toward me. "Have you been practicing your fire?"

I shook my head. I hadn't practiced at all since the girl had shown up. There was no way my power should have increased that much so suddenly.

"How do you feel?"

"Fine." I held up my hands, wondering if I should try to do it again.

Reading my intention, Ruby shouted, "No!" She pointed

49

out into the night. "Please, Freya, if you must, then do it away from here."

Everything in a ten-foot radius was singed. "Sorry."

I started off in the direction Ruby had pointed, and Chevelle joined me before I'd gone two paces. He walked beside me in silence, and when we were much more than a safe distance from the others, he halted.

I stopped as well, giving myself a few extra steps. I couldn't place his mood as I glanced over my shoulder at him, so I simply faced forward and took a steadying breath. Through squinted eyes, I watched, holding my hands out to release the flame. The size and power of it was astonishing, and it hadn't even tired me. I turned back to Chevelle trying to gauge his reaction.

I thought his expression was hopeful. Or maybe he was just trying not to laugh. It was hard to tell. "How do you feel?" he asked. His features were lit only by sparse moonlight, filtered as it was by clouds.

"Good." I smiled. And then I felt like a fool, so I straightened to match his posture.

That almost made him chuckle. He stepped toward me.

I froze.

We were alone, and he'd positioned himself squarely in front of me, not even an arm's length away. He didn't speak—he merely gazed into my eyes as if he was searching for someone. *For her.* I was close enough that I could see, even in the dark, the faint line across his chin that years ago was a scar. He was so familiar, so much a part of my other life, that it was painful.

At that moment, standing alone in the night, I remembered touching him. I recalled looking at his strong hands and placing my fingers on his. So I did.

Before I could process what had happened, his other hand was pulling me closer for a desperate kiss.

His mouth was warm against mine, his grip drawing me up to meet his height. I melted into him, relishing the sensation of his touch, of the closeness I'd been trying to reach for so long. It lasted only a moment before he realized his mistake and gauged from my response that I wasn't her, that the touch must have been merely a coincidence. He drew back to look at me again as he asked softly, almost in a whisper, "Who are you?"

I only shook my head, but he understood. He pulled his hand free of mine, and I was suddenly ashamed—I had no excuse for my actions. I'd tricked him into thinking I was someone else.

But I had remembered that touch. I glanced back at Chevelle. "What's happening?"

His face was pained, but he didn't have time to answer before Grey and Anvil's voices echoed through the darkness. Chevelle took a step away from me as we awaited their approach.

My head spun. The three of them started an apparently serious conversation, but I couldn't keep up with any of it. I merely followed them, massaging my temples as we made our way back to the camp. Steed was still near the girl, but he was quiet. Ruby had my blankets out, and I went straight to them, lay down, and closed my eyes.

It was hard to find escape from the torment of my own mind.

∼

MY DREAMS WERE CONFUSING. They were almost all about

Chevelle, but some were horrifying and some were not. I dreamt of the touch, of *before*, but the dream included our kiss from hours ago. I dreamt of things fantastic and impossible. I had some of the old dreams as well, clinging to him as we rode away from the flames with tears and ash smearing my cheeks. There was the dream of the cliff too. I stood, looking out across the horizon, and he stepped beside me, placing his hand at the small of my back. But when he shoved me off the ledge, instead of me flailing the entire way down, wings spread out and caught the air, and I took flight, soaring in the empty expanse, free.

I woke to laughter and was irritated to find them surrounding *her* again.

I rode in silence through the day, savoring a couple of the better dreams.

Once we reached the base of the mountain, the terrain turned to level ground. The trees were wiry and jagged, but they were trees nonetheless, and there was grass. Instead of feeling relief at the more familiar landscape, I found myself wondering how big a mistake I'd made by leaving the castle.

We stopped for the evening under the sparse shelter of a patch of those trees. It was warmer, so I excused myself to change out of my heavy leather boots and wool pants and into something a little more suitable. I opened my bag to find that Ruby had packed me only black with leather or silver accents —I was Lord of the North, after all. *So much for something light. At least it isn't all wool.*

I threw on the first pants I found, switched my shirt, and laced the lightest corset over it. Draping the cloak over my arm, I walked back to the camp, muttering the entire way about the redhead in charge of my wardrobe.

I was already in a foul mood, so when I saw them, I had to bite the inside of my cheek to keep from cursing. Steed was sitting opposite the human, so close that it was nearly indecent. I focused on walking to my bags across the camp from them and putting my cloak and pack away. I took as long as I could, but eventually, I had to join the group. I thought I tasted blood.

I tried not to look at them, I really did. But he touched her cheek with the back of his hand, and she flushed. He grinned at her wickedly. It was the last thing I was sure of.

What happened next didn't make any sense. I was across the camp, looking at him, but I wasn't. I could see myself in the periphery, and my head screamed with pain. Steed moved across my line of sight as I swayed, and blackness came as my eyes closed.

When they opened again, my head throbbed, with a duller version of the knifepoint pain from earlier. Back in my spot, I tried to focus, staring at Steed and the girl, but something was wrong. She had fainted. I concentrated harder and discovered Ruby staring at me accusingly.

"What?" I asked, automatically defensive.

Her eyes narrowed. She suspected *I'd* done something to the girl.

I should. But then I looked back at Steed and the human, and suddenly I understood. I *had*—I'd been in her head, just like the birds.

The pain of it was horrible, and the girl was only just coming to. When they helped her sit up, she looked frail and exhausted. Her thin hands trembled, clutching at her cloak to wrap it tightly around herself.

I lay back and covered my head to think, or maybe *not* to think.

I was asleep so fast, I might have blacked out. My dreams were darkness. Swirling blackness surrounded me. Suddenly, there were voices. One was familiar, though I couldn't place who it belonged to. "They are like witless animals... weak...

She could get through to them... Think of the possibilities..."

I knew he was talking about me, comparing me to a witless beast, an animal. Anger flooded me. The darkness turned to water as I struggled to reach the surface, unable to breathe, drowning.

I woke with a gasp, expecting to find Ruby there, watching me. What I saw instead was almost as shocking as the dreams.

"There, there." Steed brushed my bangs from my face.

I jerked away from his touch.

"Rough one, was it?"

I had the strangest feeling that he was teasing me. I must have managed to glare at him, because he laughed.

Sitting up gingerly, I looked for Ruby and Chevelle. They were several yards away, watching me but pretending not to. I wanted to groan when I saw Chevelle's tight jaw.

I wrapped my arms around my knees to bury my head. As I fully awoke, I wondered whether Steed had been teasing me all along, trying to irritate me for fun. He surely had no real interest in that human girl. I cursed the thought trying to surface that *I* was part human.

There was so much else to worry about, and it was unfathomable how I could have such distaste for someone simply because she was so like me. I lifted my eyes just enough to peer over my forearms, looking for the girl. I found her sitting with her puppy, as far away as from me as she could possibly be while remaining inside the camp.

No, I decided, *she is not like me.*

Out of the corner of my eye, I noticed the crook in Steed's lip as he watched me scrutinize her. I glared at him in response, but he only shook his head as he got up and trotted across camp to play with the puppy. I vowed not to give him the satisfaction of watching them.

But apparently, I wasn't one to hold to my word. Because when I saw him close to her, talking low and calling her my sunny nicknames, I found myself acting without regard to dignity.

Everyone in the camp turned to stare in astonishment as the small blond girl smacked Steed heartily across the face. I had already been focused on them. I had only a moment to enjoy it before the pain came again. My vision swam, my head pounding and ears ringing so that I couldn't focus on anything else. I lay my head down, and when I was finally about to open my eyes, Ruby was beside me.

The girl was sitting alone, looking completely confused and ashamed, rubbing her temples. Steed was standing across the camp, talking to Grey with his back toward me but angled enough that I could just see the edge of a bright red welt on his cheek.

I smiled with satisfaction as I let my eyes fall closed again.

I WAS quiet for the next few days. My attack seemed to have quelled the others' interest in the human, and I couldn't deny that it offered at least some relief. Silence was the easiest way to mask my contentment.

They would have to find a way to be rid of her soon, though I'd not heard any more discussion on the matter. I tried not to wonder how much longer I had before we found the council, or they us. I could see a few of them in my resurfacing memories, but I couldn't recall their names or anything about them—only random images had returned. I hadn't mentioned it to anyone because it seemed hardly worth the commotion it caused. Commotion made my head ache.

As we kept riding, the grass thickened, and the trees began

to look more like those of the village, though not nearly as large without the assistance of a light elf's magic. We'd stopped near a pond to camp, and I was considering taking a dip as Ruby took the girl for her evening's privacy. The men gathered nearby, talking in hushed voices. I decided it wasn't worth eavesdropping and having myself act the fool again, so I looked out over the water, watching the dragonflies bounce just above the glassy surface.

The days had become warmer, but the evenings felt more of my new home in the mountains. It was cool and dark in the castle where I had apparently been raised. Even though I couldn't remember that time, there was comfort in the night that brought a relief from the heat and brightness that devoured the southern lands. As the sunlight faded, I sat on a rock near the water, and it was cool enough that I could close my eyes and almost pretend I'd never left the safety of the castle.

The group's discussion became heated, and I absentmindedly turned toward them. My eyes caught a flicker of movement in a tree line several yards behind them. Suddenly, Chevelle was gone, and Steed and Grey were posted in front of me protectively before I even had the chance to see what— or who—the movement was.

I couldn't understand why we hadn't heard the wolves signal. Panic flooded through me as I remembered the battle from before. The feeling of being tied to that wall and stabbed through with thorns as my mind was attacked was indelible.

Someone had come for us. For me.

I tried to calm down. Even if it was the worst I could imagine, if it was Council, that was who we were looking for. I cursed myself again for insisting that I come along. The seconds dragged as I waited.

After what felt like a few eternities, I recognized Junnie's voice. She was speaking with Chevelle in a rush, her tone low. As they drew near, Steed and Grey relaxed slightly in front of me, Grey stepping a pace to the side. I had been moved to standing. Steed's arm was so close that it was almost touching me as he stood half in front of me. I stared past him, the tension in his muscles making me wonder why he was still protecting me.

Then I remembered that Junnie wasn't just my tutor and friend. She was Council. She was my mother's aunt. My head swam, and I clutched Steed's arm in an attempt to focus. I had no idea how to react to her. She was still speaking to Chevelle in a flood of words that ran together. She hadn't even seemed to notice me.

When she finally looked in my direction, it was not at me or my guards. I barely had time to turn and see Ruby approaching before it happened. The spots in my vision came just as fast. Through them, I saw a flash of Junnie's cloak flying past as she picked up the limp body of the human girl, and then they were gone.

5

I SHOULD HAVE CAUGHT ON BY THEN THAT THE FAINTING WAS A protective mechanism, but I didn't always think rationally, and shock wasn't an easily controlled reaction. The bonds that held my mind captive shut down my body every time I struggled to get free. They refused to let me break out of the spells tangled within, tightening their hold with every strike I made, every stress I tried to endure. I fought them anyway, and I was barely able to hang on. It had taken me to my knees, but I wouldn't let it take me further, no matter the cost.

Before my eyes opened, I heard someone speaking: "The pup as well..." Recognition came, and then confusion returned. Junnie had seen the girl—the human—and her reaction was fierce, even worse than my own. I'd heard a low oath just before the girl's body had collapsed, hitting the ground with a chilling hollow thud. Junnie hadn't even waited for an explanation of who the girl was or why she was with us. If I'd only been able to tell her, I might have saved the girl.

My blood went cold. I hadn't even tried.

I lost my focus then, despite my resolve. My eyelids fluttered as the blackness came, leaving me with nothing but dreams.

I WAS in the practice rooms. A tall, dark-haired man with a long scar across his brow was threatening me, pushing me too far. Darkness creeped closer and closer, surrounding us. Then I felt alone in the gloom as it swirled around me, but I couldn't have been truly alone—I heard voices. My chest tightened as I realized what the voices were saying about me. They compared me to them, calling me a witless beast. It ached. *How could he?* I didn't understand. I ran to my mother. She had been right.

I AWOKE LONG before I could bear to open my eyes. When I did, everyone was quiet. I didn't question them, and I'd forgotten about the girl, about Junnie. All I could think of was the dream. It couldn't have been right. My grandfather had been killed in the massacre, and he hadn't ruled since. He *must* have been gone, but the man in my dream—Lord Asher, my mother's father, the one who had driven her to the massacre, the man who had pushed us both—was not gone.

I could not fathom how that man could have possibly been the same Asher who had met with Chevelle when Chevelle had been gathering the others—my guard—at Ruby's.

I remembered the first time I had seen the dark-haired man and the look he'd given me, the way his knuckles whitened as he gripped the staff, his shabby cloak. I remembered thinking it must have been a disguise because of the way he carried himself, then chastising myself for being so paranoid.

I realized I was staring at Chevelle as I recalled their meeting. He was watching me with concern on his face, and a thought flashed through my mind that maybe he knew I was on to him. It was all so wrong.

My head spun, and I closed my eyes, trying to find something to grasp, something to steady me before I blacked out again. I needed a way to fix the conflict. Asher couldn't have been my grandfather. It could not be true. I struggled to sit up long enough to reach my pack. I felt around for it, the only real thing I had. My fingers caught the edge of the binding, and I pulled the diary out, clutching it tightly, as if someone might try to take it from me.

I couldn't make myself look at the others, but I knew what they were thinking: that this was it, that I was finally falling into madness. It was a few moments before I could focus well enough to read. I flipped through the first pages, where my mother wrote as a child, her father's prize.

A tear tracked down my cheek, and I wiped at it distractedly. When I felt their eyes on me, I hardened, biting down, determined to keep another from escaping. I did not want pity, not from anyone.

I scanned, searching for mention of him, but I kept getting caught in the story. It was all so different now that it wasn't a stranger's. It was my mother's story, my story. *And Asher's?*

Page after page, I kept my nose buried in the diary. No one asked me to move, but they kept close. I could feel them watching, waiting. They were concerned about what had broken free inside of me and if it would be the thing that pushed me over the edge. Eventually, exhaustion won out, and the dreams were back.

BY THE NEXT DAY, I was almost certain that the dreams were not simply dreams—they were memories, and the Asher I had seen was in fact *Lord* Asher. What I could not reconcile was how he was alive, how he could have met with Chevelle, and why.

My thoughts were clearer, but that made them all the more distressing. It felt as though secrets were everywhere, swallowing me. It felt as if I was drowning, and the sensation was all too familiar.

I recalled more each time I encountered him. I focused on the day he had watched us from the tree line, the day I'd felt untethered from my own soul, remembering how they had reacted to his single nod and his seeming approval. I could see his braid swing behind him as he turned and disappeared into the brush. I struggled to understand, and I couldn't help but remember what had happened just before, a memory I'd not returned to willingly: the sickening thud as the council tracker's head landed on the ground, the sight of it rolling to a stop, and the blood on my blade.

Yet I could not understand, so I forced myself to stop thinking about it. It was the only way to put an end to the screeching pain in my head, to save me from the blackouts. However, when I finally calmed the searing pain to a dull throb, I could begin to feel the ache in my chest. It was tough to breathe. *How could they...* I couldn't even finish the thought before the other pain returned. I was balancing, and not well, on a narrow ledge.

Betrayal. Chaos. Loss. Madness.

It was some time later that I broke, unable to stand the conflict in my own mind or the pain it was causing me. *The pain they were causing me? No, I can't allow myself to think that.*

When I finally gave, I found solace in the mind of the hawk as it hovered above us, floating on the current of the wind. I stayed there, void of all other thoughts until, exhausted, I had to surrender and return to my own body.

IN TIME, I found a compromise with myself. I would let go of the other concerns when possible and devote my concentration to the one thing I was positive of: we—no, *I* needed to find Council, to release my mind from the bonds that felt like they were killing me. I could only hope that doing so would release the memories as well, remove all of the unanswered questions, and erase the doubt that was constantly trying to creep into every thought I had. *How could they? And always, why?*

Finally, I was in control of myself enough to continue. Our task became my first priority: find Council. I focused on my memories of them, the images of their faces. It was all I had, but at least it was something.

Ruby scrutinized me, obviously concerned as we rode through a field of tall grass. I ignored her, pretending to watch my horse steal bites along the way, struggling to keep a steady pace as his head bent sideways, securing generous mouthfuls.

She couldn't stand it for long. "Frey?"

I looked at her blankly. Her eyes went wide, my gaze apparently not as blank as I'd intended. I tried to smooth it. "Hmm?"

She must not have planned for my response, because she said nothing, her expression tortured. I wondered what she was reading on mine.

She glanced forward at the backs of the others as they rode

ahead of us then at me. "Was there something specific you were looking for in the diary?"

It struck me that she had no idea why I had been reading it again. I had not mentioned my dream or my new knowledge. She must have thought that I'd been upset about Junnie or the human. They must have all thought that. They had no idea that I had remembered anything new.

I realized that I was smiling. Some part of me, buried deep inside, was pleased. It relished the secret knowledge and wanted to protect it. It was not a pleasant character trait, I supposed, and not the first negative quality I'd found in myself. I spoke without thinking. "No, it was just a shock. I'm fine."

Her eyebrows knitted together.

"I'd been meaning to finish reading it. You know, for closure." I almost scoffed at my own words. She was staring at me hard, so I changed the subject. "So, where exactly are we going?"

It didn't appear as though I'd lessened her concern, but she looked forward and nodded at some structure in the distance. Tied up in my thoughts, I hadn't even noticed it.

We rode closer, and the shapes became more defined. I kicked up my horse to fall in beside the others for a better view. In a ring of yew trees, pillars of stone rose up in patterns around a massive amphitheater.

I gulped, cringing at the thought of what the place could be. "Grand Council?" I whispered.

"No," Anvil answered, smiling.

I let out a breath, the tightness in my chest easing by degrees.

Chevelle spoke from the front. "The Temple of Loelle."

Once I could see more clearly, it was apparent that the structure had been abandoned long ago. Here and there, the sandstone pillars crumbled at their corners, gangly weeds spiking up between the footstones. Faint outlines of carvings bordered the base of the columns, weathered away with time. The others stopped and dismounted, leaving the horses as they entered the central building. I followed behind, still cautious. I remembered my plan to sweep the sky each day—I'd forgotten that during the time spent agonizing over Asher—and I had to catch myself to focus on the present.

A light dusting of sand shifted beneath my feet, making me feel a bit more secure in my abandonment theory. Regardless of my concerns about the group's relationship with Asher, I was glad they were there. I knew I would be unable to stand alone to face Grand Council when the time came—soon.

I shivered, and Chevelle moved beside me, his hand sliding across my back. It did not ease the chill inside me, and I had to force myself not to look at him to avoid betraying my emotions.

"We will stay here until Rhys and Rider can locate Council."

Some part of me expected to stiffen at his words, but I became aware that I already was—I had hardened when he'd first touched me. He must have noticed, too, because he dropped his arm as he continued. "You will need to train."

He turned and walked off without another word, but as if on command, Anvil approached, holding two large metal rods.

We trained through the evening as the others gathered in small groups, planning, watching, or checking the perimeter. I was exhausted when we finally stopped for dinner, and almost before I'd finished my last bite, Grey was urging me to train again, to practice trying to stop his disappearing acts. It was well past dark when I finally gave up.

～

THOUGH I'D FALLEN asleep by the fire, I awoke inside my own small hut, complete with soft bedding. I dragged myself from the cot, only to find the day's training already planned for me. "Let's go," said Ruby. "We'll work on your control today."

I managed not to groan aloud, but internally I was doing more than my share of complaining.

"Now!" she shouted. "Here!"

That pattern continued, in the middle of that strange temple between nothing but forest and grass. Ruby drove me during the waking hours, her fire lighting around me so often that it swam through my vision even when my eyes were closed. Grey's training had me moving constantly, always too slow to catch his strikes. "Focus," they would command, as if it was even within my control.

By the third day, exhaustion was winning out. They pushed me relentlessly. I was too tired even to be miserable. It reminded me of something that I couldn't quite place, when I'd been forced to train, exhausted, and paranoid.

I cried out in defeat as Ruby's whip cracked at my shoulder. I fell to my knees, spent.

"Up!" she commanded.

I huffed out a breath, having no intention of following her order.

She stepped forward, her gaze trained on mine. "Up."

I forced a look of defiance, and her expression became heated.

"You will burn, Frey."

Not by her hand, by Council's. I convinced myself to stand, not for her but for me, to give myself every possible chance when the time came. On wobbly legs, I fought back.

When I could stand no more, it was Anvil's turn, but I didn't have much left to fight off electrical attacks.

On the fourth night, a new dream surfaced.

It was twisted and confusing, but I came away with an unmistakable feeling. I stayed inside my hut, pretending to sleep, and pulled the diary from my pack. I flipped forward to the pages in which my mother described her own training. Asher, her father, had forced her to train for his own benefit.

I was certain of their actions. The idea that had been nagging at me grew until it was fully formed. They weren't training me for my protection—I had no chance against Council in my condition. And it wasn't merely to keep me occupied. They were training me for Lord Asher.

I gritted my teeth against the hate that was filling me.

"Frey?" a voice asked from outside the hut.

The part of me that had relished my secret knowledge was in control again. I took a calming breath before answering, "Yes, Ruby?"

"We should probably get started."

I took two more deep breaths. "All right."

I stood, trying to get a handle on the tremor that was racking my body and praying that the madness would not split me in two. With one more deep breath, I stepped out into the sun.

I tried to keep my expression clear as I scanned the temple. I remembered Anvil before. He'd been in some of the older memories, helping the scarred man with training—no, practice. I continued, seeing Grey and Steed by a pillar. I couldn't decide on their involvement. They might have just been there for Ruby.

Ruby was the troublemaker—*could that be why she's involved? Merely for fun, her own entertainment?* Then I remembered what Steed had said: her interest in the diary was because of her mother. I wondered if revenge or some sick obsession because her fey mother had come up with a crazed plan because of me was driving her.

"Frey?" Ruby sounded concerned. She wrapped her hand around my arm, pulling me to focus on her. "Frey, what is it?" She sounded panicked, and I realized I was shaking again.

A strange part of me needed to cover for us. I couldn't think clearly, so I spat out the first reasonable truth I could give. "I-I just remembered something."

She waited.

"Council... a council member."

"Who?"

"I don't know. I only see his face. Nothing else."

She nodded and rubbed my arm. I played on her sympathy, and eventually she encouraged me to lie back down.

When I was alone again, the rush of thought and emotion tore through me. I struggled to hold myself together. I had no one but these seven companions. I didn't want to believe they would betray me, but I could not otherwise explain their association with Asher, the man who had ruined my mother, the North, and me. A wave of nausea hit, and I doubled over, sweat thick on my brow. I tried to wipe it away with a shaky hand, but found I needed to grip the cot to keep from falling. My eyes closed as dizziness took over. Someone was coming in, and I became aware that I had been moaning in agony.

I heard them talking. "What's wrong with her?"

"Get Ruby."

A few moments later, Chevelle's voice rang out. His betrayal hurt the worst. It pushed me over the edge, past that breaking point I'd been fighting so hard not to pass, and I couldn't focus on their words or find feeling in my limbs. I could only recognize the burning of my skin and the pain in my mind. Something was wrong, and it was much worse than before. I shut down completely.

~

FEVER DROVE my dreams to new heights. More irrational paranoia seeped through all of my old dreams, turning them to nightmares, but the new ones were most disturbing. Even the colors frightened me. Blood red and flame orange saturated everything in one moment, and then stark white swallowed me whole.

My companions, my guard, surrounded me in the long robes and tassels of Grand Council. Chevelle approached me, his face hard. As he closed in, his mouth twisted in a menacing grin, and he grabbed me, pulling me close for a deep kiss. When he drew away, I tasted blood. Then fire lit around me, and they gathered to watch me burn.

I wanted to scream, but my throat was grated raw by the fine sand of the surrounding pillars. The flames threw wicked shadows across the ground, which began to sway, and I lost my footing, falling down only to be kicked by the watchers. I laughed then, crazed by the flame, and I could feel my mother. I knew she too had laughed as she burned, and I began to scream.

MY OWN HOARSE scream woke me. I started up in a panic, but Ruby held me down, patting my forehead with a damp bit of cloth. I was drenched, shivering as my eyelids fluttered before falling back to closed.

They must have thought I was asleep again, as a groggy relaxation kept me still. I could hear their whispers as I silently took stock. "Maybe that's not even why… Maybe we overdid the training… No, let her rest…"

My body seemed to have recovered. My mind was rested but still in pain. I tried not to think of why, wanting to stave off the worst of the pains in case it was the bindings.

They gave me the rest of the day off, but that evening, after Ruby had brought me dinner, the makeshift door to my room was tossed open, and Chevelle stood there, staring at me. His impatience seared me through his tone. "Enough. Get up. Return to your training."

For just a moment, I was surprised. Then, in a flash of anger, I found myself responding without thought. "Why? For him?" I couldn't stop myself. That secret part of me that had better control was nowhere to be found. "How could you? After what he did. How?"

A small group had gathered behind Chevelle, seeking the source of the commotion. It only enflamed me more.

"All of you. My guard," I spat. They stared at me as though I had lost it, and maybe I had. "Training me at his command. Slaves to Asher. Your *Lord* Asher."

I had directed that last part to Chevelle, and his face went white. He wore an expression that I had never seen, and honestly, it frightened me. I ran from the hut, tearing brush free of the back wall to get away from them as fast as I could.

Breathless and with no idea where to go, I kept running until my shaking legs would carry me no farther.

Apparently, it wasn't far enough. When I finally rose from the ground to look behind me, Ruby was already there. I was pretty sure she'd been right behind me the entire time, silent. She appeared annoyed with her mouth turned down and a fist perched on a hip.

I turned my head away from her and dropped it to the ground. She let me stay there until eventually, I gave in and followed her back to the temple. I might have been embarrassed by my outburst, but no one had denied my accusations, so I felt justified, wronged, and bitter.

The fever was gone, so I continued to practice through that bitterness. No matter their reasons for training me, I knew I would not be able to face Grand Council without them, and they knew it too. I could only work to get better. Then I would worry about the others, about Asher, and about how I would have to face things alone.

～

NIGHTS LATER, I woke with a start, remembering that I had abandoned my plan of sweeping the area. I knew Rhys and Rider were on guard with the wolves, but I hadn't forgotten the last time, when Council had bested them. I hoped I could locate a vessel as I closed my eyes and searched past the temple and the pillars into the surrounding trees.

An owl perched in a red oak near the temple, and I decided he would suffice. I started to take him off his branch to check the grounds when his keen eyes caught a group standing together not far from his spot. Focusing, I realized it was Anvil and Grey, close together and speaking, and Chevelle, who faced away from them with his arms crossed, giving his stance an irritated feel.

I was afraid to move any nearer, sure the flapping of wings would alert them. I considered checking for other animals close by but imagined Chevelle spotting a clumsy squirrel with his knowing eyes, catching me spying. The uncoordinated squirrel was taking over my thoughts, and I had to focus and try not to chuckle at my sleepy efforts.

I concentrated, finally hearing their words, but just as I caught them—"Fannie's doing our job"—Chevelle spun, facing them, his anger palpable. Grey held up his hands as if to say "no harm," but it didn't matter—Chevelle was beyond calming. When he scanned the clearing, I jumped back into my own mind, afraid that he'd somehow known I was there.

I couldn't fall asleep after that. I couldn't understand what they'd meant or why they were talking about Fannie. I wondered what they'd been referring to as their "job" and if it was something they were doing for Asher. But I couldn't fathom how Fannie could be doing that. She wasn't training me. It had to be something else, then. Maybe they had more than one task.

"What is it?" Ruby asked from the corner. I hadn't noticed her. She was apparently watching me even during peaceful sleep now.

I started to answer that it was nothing but decided, given my previous outburst when I gave the secret away, that I might as well ask. "Fannie," I said, sitting up to face her.

She leaned forward. "What about Fannie?"

I wasn't sure how to respond. She didn't know what I did or didn't remember, what I did or didn't know. I wanted to find a way to lead her into answers.

"Frey, did you see Fannie?"

Evidently, it was going to be easier than I thought. I remembered the dream and used that. She could decide what to do with it. "Destroying the village."

In the dim light, I saw Ruby's reaction, and I knew that it hadn't been a dream at all. I gasped, choking on the shock.

She moved to sit beside me on the cot, and in my stupor, I let her attempt to comfort me. "Freya, I'm sorry."

My skin crawled at the endearment. "Don't call me that."

She was stunned at my response. "I'm sorry I didn't tell you before. It's just that I know what it does to you when you get upset."

"As if you care," I spat.

The surprise in her expression twisted to hurt. "Frey—"

"Oh, come on, Ruby. You work for Asher. You read the diary. You know—"

"You..." She stopped herself. "Elfreda, you are the most

ridiculous…" I didn't know what she intended to call me, but she grabbed my arms tightly and stared me straight in the eye before she started again. "I. Do. Not. Work. For. Anyone." She released her grip just a fraction. "Is that clear?"

I had no idea what my face gave away, but my mind was anything but clear.

She rumbled out an irritated growl. "Listen to me. If that is what you're thinking, then there is no danger of telling you now. I don't see how it could possibly make things worse for you." She took off on a side rant. "And all this time, I thought you were upset about that stupid girl!"

Guilt washed through me again as I remembered the human.

Ruby continued, "Frey, Fannie is after Grand Council."

My mouth dropped open. "What?"

"She's killing them."

I couldn't get my voice to work.

Ruby continued in a softer tone, "She was bound. Same as you."

Pain racked my mind, but I tried to stay focused.

She recounted the binding. "She was not considered guilty, as your mother was, and she was allowed to live, though bound tightly and under watch. You see, when we fought them before, as we tried to release your bonds… we inadvertently released some of hers as well."

My chest tightened, but I couldn't convince myself it was real. "How do you know?"

She looked at me as though I was missing something. I didn't see it. "Junnie."

Junnie. I'd never even wondered why she'd come or what she'd spoken to Chevelle about in such a rush before saw the girl. The cursed bonds kept me from facing anything, kept my mind in a constant maelstrom that pulled me under when the turmoil became too much. "Focus," they said, as if that wasn't the very thing that did me in. I still couldn't speak.

"I should let you rest for a bit. Are you going to be all right?"

"No," I begged. "Please, Ruby, tell me more." She didn't think I could handle it—I could see that. I probably couldn't, but it didn't stop me. "Ruby, I need to know."

"What do you want to know?" She hedged.

I wasn't sure where to start. My thoughts were in that current, and it was too strong to conquer. "Why? Why did she destroy the village?"

"We think she blamed them for the binding." Ruby shrugged. "Or maybe she just loathed them. Hard to say."

I shook my head. "Why would she blame them?"

"Somehow, apparently, she'd gotten parts of her magic back, and she was confused, though she knew for sure that she'd been bound."

I thought of my time with Fannie, her conspiracy theories and her hatred of all things Council. "How long had she known?"

"We can't be certain. She was secretive and probably didn't know who to trust. We don't think she knew of Junnie's involvement, though." Ruby looked sorry that she had mentioned Junnie. She straightened the edge of my blanket. "However, she did seem to know you were bound as well. At least at the end, just before you left the village."

"How did she know?" I ignored the dance she'd done around my choking a council leader and running off after I'd been accused of practicing dark magic. At the time, I'd had no idea.

"We aren't sure, but the documents you found had been taken from Council. And the ones that you"—there was really no other way to say it—"stole had been tampered with."

"Tampered with?"

"Mixed up, at the least. Unfortunately, we didn't get a good look at them before—"

"Before I burned them."

"Yes." Ruby attempted a timid smile.

"So you think Fannie used me to get the documents? Or do you mean she tried to frame me to get me into trouble with Council?" I could hear my voice shake.

"There is no way to know what she was thinking or what she was after, Frey. From what I understand, there was no love lost there." She touched my hand sympathetically.

I struggled to remember, but it seemed so far away, and none were memories I'd wanted to cherish. Something came to me, and I couldn't help but ask, since Ruby was being open with me. I pushed down the thought that was trying to scream maybe she wasn't being honest—maybe it was more lies. Instead of asking directly about the spell that placed the map on my palms or having to recount my dream of the trick we'd played on Fannie, I took a side route. "Ruby, what about the pouch? Did she know I had that?"

Ruby shook her head. "I don't know much about that, Frey. But I do know one thing: the silver medallion, the one you found inside, seems to match those that Fannie had secured from the human site you read about in your mother's diary."

I swallowed hard, wondering when Ruby had seen the medallion. In the castle, probably, maybe during one of the many times I'd been unconscious. I'd had no idea what the symbols meant, but I'd never made the connection to—it was still hard to think—*humans*. I pushed on. "And the ruby?"

She seemed almost embarrassed as she answered this time. "Yes. You see, that was payment. Please understand, that was before I knew you."

"Payment?" I was incredulous, but she only nodded. "Payment for what?"

"Securing some items, helping you, gathering the guard."

Bitter resentment wanted to rise, fire was waiting in my palms, and the ache was heavy in my chest, but I kept them all still. Some part of me needed the rest of the secret, in spite of everything. I hadn't forgotten her words from just moments ago: *I do not work for anyone.*

Lies. All of it was lies.

Ruby could see that I'd had enough. She moved aside as I rolled away from her to curl into a ball.

And, after a few hours of mental torment, I fell asleep thinking I had reached my limit and feeling certain that I was beyond surprise.

6

SOMEWHERE IN THE DEPTHS OF MY SUBCONSCIOUS, I KNEW THAT what I was watching might finally crack me, leaving me in separate pieces. But I couldn't make myself look away.

From a perch above, I could see Fannie slinking slowly toward a council member. He stood tall, his robe and tassels unruffled, murmuring words I could not understand. I couldn't decide whether to scream in warning or to root for his demise, for I knew that his death would release me.

The panther came into his view and sauntered closer, enjoying itself far too much. Then without warning, it launched forward into the chest of the council member Magnus White. It tore out his throat as they both landed on the ground, blood spattering down his clean white robe, tassels splaying out behind him.

The cat lingered above its prey, savoring the sight of blood flowing from the fatal wound. Then it turned, slowly and deliberately, to look directly at me, its dark muzzle wet with death.

Fear overtook me.

I WOKE to my own words, oblivious at first to my surroundings. "The animals. She's using the animals."

As a hand touched my shoulder, I realized I wasn't alone—Ruby and Chevelle were in my tattered shelter. My chest heaved, and Ruby tried to calm me. "Easy, Frey."

They had been watching me sleep, likely waiting because they wanted to talk to me. Ruby had probably explained our conversation about Fannie to him. A shiver racked my body.

"What is it, Frey?" Ruby asked, her tone concerned as her hand remained resting on my shoulder. From across the shelter, Chevelle's gaze narrowed as he gave her a knowing look. He must have blamed her for telling me, knowing my mind wouldn't be able to handle it.

I shook my head and sat up straighter. "She's using the cats." Even in my panic, I regretted that I had chosen cats for my own ploy in the castle. "She's taking Council out, one by one. She knows."

He stiffened. "How could you know that?"

I didn't answer his question, instead rambling about my dream. "She knows they won't kill the animals, knows she has free rein to slaughter all the council members if she uses beasts." I could hear the blind panic in my own voice.

He leaned forward. "Frey, it was only a dream. No one knows—"

"No," I cut him off. "I *know*. And she's coming after me."

My thoughts were frantic. Fannie understood that the light elves had reverence for nature and rules about killing animals. She knew they wouldn't fight back when she was in that form, not hard enough to truly stop her. And I was next. She was coming for me. I strived to hold on, to not let the chaos in my mind drive me mad. But I was swaying back and forth, curling my fists.

Eventually, the motion calmed, and rational thought returned. The further I got from sleep, the more the dream lost its potency. Ruby sat beside me, offering me tea and powders and anything else she could think of. It was quiet for a long time when I refused.

Then it struck me that they were too quiet. They weren't shocked at all. "You knew?"

Ruby didn't answer, and I looked at Chevelle accusingly for what seemed like the hundredth time.

"We could not be certain."

How? How could they have known? "Junnie?"

He replied with a curt nod.

I started to demand why they hadn't told me that my crazed aunt was coming to murder me, but as my mouth opened, I remembered the chain of events that had followed Junnie's visit. They couldn't have explained anything to me—I'd passed out, and when I awoke, I didn't speak. I'd been obsessed, doing nothing except reading the diary of my dead mother. They thought I was too fragile to include.

I closed my mouth, curling my fingers into sweating palms. *They might have been right.* I blew out a shaky breath. *Fannie is killing Council.* I felt like a complete fool.

"That's why I'm remembering." It seemed so obvious now. All I received was another nod. Just like Ruby had said, as we broke my bonds, we were breaking hers... and she was breaking mine.

Grey came to the opening in the shelter, and Ruby stepped out to speak with him. I watched her leave and kept my gaze on the doorway. I was alone with Chevelle.

The air was charged, as it always was when I was alone with him. *Always thick with anger or—*I stopped myself, embarrassed by the thought of how I'd acted the last time he'd been in my shelter. I had accused him of working for Asher.

I couldn't even think clearly anymore—there was so much wrong in my head. It was impossible to be rational or control my emotions with so much missing and disconnected. I let myself look at him.

It was a mistake.

He had been watching me, his gaze already trained on my face. I felt off-balance and briefly wondered if Ruby had drugged me again because without a conscious command to do so, I found myself moving toward him.

He was sitting near the end of my cot, on the stool where Ruby had watched me sleep. I felt how small the room was as I slid down to sit next to him in the dimness. I couldn't stop myself from wanting to be near him, no matter how wrong it seemed. I was entirely confused—I felt as though I knew him and he was part of my life, but at the same time, he was a stranger, mysterious in every way. I forgot all those strong feelings of betrayal as I sat inches away from him, looking into his eyes.

He was staring expectantly at me, but all I could see was a memory, a similar situation when his face was filled with something else, sadness or disappointment. I couldn't seem to pull it to mind, couldn't find the clear, solid memory, and I was overcome with frustration. My hands came up, knotting in my hair as the base of my palms pressed against my temples. I could feel myself rocking back and forth again, but I was too overwhelmed to stop.

Suddenly, I was jerked from the bed to standing. At first, my eyes shot to Chevelle's hand on my wrist. His grip was so tight that it was almost painful. But when I realized he'd pulled me close to him, our bodies nearly touching, my eyes slowly trailed to his face.

But he wasn't looking at me. I opened my mouth to speak, and he reached up, placing his fingers on my lips to still them. His head was turned away as he listened intently, so I concentrated to hear what had his attention. It was distant and slightly muffled, a strange sort of noise. Then the pitch rose, and I realized it was animals. Within seconds, a clearer sound came: the wolves sounded a warning cry.

I was wrenched from the tent so quickly that I could barely keep my footing. I tumbled forward, losing my last step, and Chevelle lifted me and ran away from the temple. Panic seized me, but I couldn't see behind us. He was intent on his path. The only way I could think of to see what was behind us— after us—was to jump to the wolves.

I managed to locate one, but even as I sensed where it was, I wasn't able to find its mind to learn why it had called out a warning. Confused, I searched for the second wolf and tried again.

Nothing. I didn't understand—it had never not worked.

"Frey." Chevelle's voice brought me back, and I opened my eyes to find his face in front of mine. We had stopped running. He gazed down at me, still in his arms. "Are you all right?"

I stared back at him. *Nothing had happened to me, had it?* I took stock, but aside from the frantic beat of my heart and labored breathing, I could find nothing wrong. I nodded to him in reply.

He put me down, and I started toward a nearby rock ledge to sit, still baffled that I'd been unable to get through to the wolves. *Was it Council? Had they bound me from the animals now?*

Chevelle must have seen my dread return as I stepped away because he grabbed my arm and drew me back to face him. "What is it?"

I couldn't answer. I knew my face had paled. They'd taken from me the one thing that made me revered.

"Frey." He gave my shoulders a quick shake to pull me back.

A small squirrel jumped from a limb in my peripheral vision, and I felt it automatically and fell into its mind with ease. Satisfied I'd not lost the ability, I finally started to relax, but my vision went black when the animal's neck snapped.

My eyes opened in time to see its body tumble to the ground. I was standing with my mouth hanging open in disbelief as Chevelle glanced back at me. Only then did I realize he'd been watching the squirrel. He had been distracted at first, but the noise had alerted him, and he'd focused on the squirrel a breath before it had dropped.

"Did you kill that squirrel?" I accused.

He answered in his careful tone, "Frey—"

The tone infuriated me, and I cut him off. "Tell me now."

He leaned back indignantly. "Did you have a personal relationship with that squirrel?"

He'd never spoken to me that way. It threw me off for half a second, and then I was incensed. "Tell me right now."

"Tell you what?"

We were suddenly arguing. I leaned forward, my hands in tight fists at my sides. "Tell me whatever it is that you're hiding from me. What now, what else?"

He twitched, the muscles of his forearm tensing. His jaw jumped too as he stared at me, tight-lipped for a long moment. Finally, he sighed and said, "We are simply taking every precaution. To protect you."

The words enraged me. "To protect me? How many times do I have to hear that? 'Oh, it's just to protect you.'" I had the perverse urge to strike him but arrested the thought. "What is it now? What are you doing to protect me now?" I spat.

He only looked at me.

I waited.

"The animals," he replied, watching me as though I'd missed something obvious again. My anger flared until I realized the implication.

The fury rushed out of me in a huff. I was as winded as if I'd been punched in the chest. I didn't understand how I could be so continuously oblivious. They were lining up in my head, the details I'd so blatantly missed. Some were more noticeable than others, but they were all there: the battle with Council, when I'd felt someone else in the mind of the bird, the glaringly obvious lack of animals on our path, and Fannie's apparent abilities, which I had seen so clearly in my dreams.

Fannie. Suddenly, my head was spinning, joining the images from my dreams with the last few hours and minutes. I was speaking before I was aware of it. "We were running."

Chevelle gripped my arm, and I knew he heard the change in my voice.

"Running from Fannie." I'd known she was coming for me. I hadn't known she was already here.

I looked into his eyes. I wasn't sure what he saw on my face, but he was abruptly trying to calm me. "Frey, she hasn't gotten near you at all."

I felt my features twist at his words.

"The wolves are taking care of them," he said.

The wolves. Taking care of them. *Not an animal,* animals. *How many times has she tried? How long has this been going on?* I opened my mouth to speak, but I couldn't process the anger and humiliation, the irritation. I growled in rage, throwing my fisted hands to my sides. The sound of shattering stone caught my attention.

I realized it had been me. I sighed, suddenly ashamed that I'd unintentionally exploded the rock ledge that had been my intended seat moments before. I loosened my fists, throwing my hands up in surrender.

I turned from Chevelle to walk toward the temple, or at least in the direction I thought it had been, unwilling to look at him. I heard his steps behind me, following my slow progress, and remembered his words from the time I had been attacked by Council, when they'd found me and rebound my magic. He'd said they had known Council was close, but they were mistaken in thinking Council intended a physical attack. They had been prepared for that, and I knew they were more than capable of defeating Council. However, they had not been prepared for the binding, the direct attack on my mind. He'd assured me that Council would not get so close again.

And now they're... what, destroying every animal that came near because Fannie was tracking me too? The wolves were my guard dogs? I was too far gone to laugh. I could see their first demonstration of power in my memory, hear their vicious snarl, see their jagged fangs. Ruby's words came back to me: *"No, silly, no one can control animals. The wolves attack who they want and protect who they want."*

I kept walking slowly over dirt and thick clumps of grass, attempting to process it all, struggling to find a place for it. Twice I spun on Chevelle, ready to fling accusations at him, but each time, his expression was such that I could only look at him before I turned and continued on.

Eventually, I came into a clearing, the hot sun directly overhead a clear indication that I'd been walking far too long. I couldn't decide if I'd passed the temple or gone in a different direction entirely. Sighing, I turned, finding Chevelle behind me, exactly where I'd expected him.

He waited.

I took a deep breath. "I don't know where I am."

His expression was pained as he took a step toward me. "I know, Frey. We are trying to help you."

I put my hands up in front of me. "No. I mean I don't know *where* I am." I waved toward the surrounding wall of trees.

He almost smiled as he took another step closer. "They will be waiting for us." Before I could respond, he pulled me up to carry me again, spinning and breaking into a run toward the temple.

I hadn't even been close.

7

ONCE I KNEW I WAS BEING HUNTED BY THE REMAINING members of Grand Council *and* my crazy Aunt Fannie in various animal forms, it was considerably easier to forgive the seven others who were willing to help me, regardless of their reasons.

It was in that state of mind that, upon returning to the temple, I resumed my training with Grey. The others were planning again, something about moving since Fannie had likely found us. I wasn't sure what "likely" meant, since the wolves had apparently slaughtered numerous beasts throughout the morning, but I ignored their discussions, confident that they would not have let me join in.

We found a quiet spot near the center of the temple. The sandstone floor was open, free of the pillars that bordered the outer walls, so I hoped I would have a better chance to follow Grey's movements as he flitted around in an attempt to lose me. Unfortunately, I was often disappointed. I readied myself, standing motionless with my eyes and ears on alert when he stepped in front of me, wearing a smile.

I scowled, certain he was making fun of me, though I had no idea why.

"I never thanked you for the assist," he said.

I was lost for a moment before I understood what he was referring to: the battle with Council. I'd missed the majority of it, at first tied to a wall then overtaken by blackness, but I had managed to fight some. A bird had flown over, and I'd jumped to it, able to see them all below in the fray. Grey had been trapped as my own body had been, vines wrapping him in place, long thorns piercing his skin, flames surrounding him. I had found his attacker and given Grey the few precious seconds he needed to escape. The horrid scene filled my mind anew, and as I looked at it with fresh knowledge, I couldn't help but wonder if they had actually been fighting to protect me.

Then the last little bit of the memory came back, the moments just before the blackness had taken me. Asher watched from outside the battle. I could see his lips moving, a flow of words.

"Frey?"

Grey had been talking to me, although I had no idea what he'd said. I answered anyway. "Yes, of course."

He laughed, and then he was gone.

I shook my head, trying to focus because I knew I was about to be smacked in the back of the head or have a leg pulled out from under me when he reappeared.

I was wrong. I got a punch in the gut. Yet to my surprise, he was still standing in front of me. We both looked down to see my hand wrapped tightly around his wrist. He was lightning fast, but I'd grabbed him somehow, almost unthinkingly.

We stood there, staring at the offending hands, unable to relax at first. Then I let loose a breath, and Grey opened his fist as I eased my grip on him.

We didn't speak.

"Frey," Ruby started as she bounced up to us. Noticing the uncomfortable atmosphere, she asked, "What's going on?"

Grey spoke up, smiling genuinely at her without looking me in the eye. "Hey, Red. Just finishing up here." He gingerly reached up to pat me on the back of the shoulder. "The girl's really picking it up. Impressive."

Ruby eyed me, perplexed. I squeaked out a nervous laugh, and she glanced back and forth between us a few times before shaking it off. "It's time to move. Frey, I'll get your things together. You can keep practicing until we have everything ready."

She threw one quick look back to Grey with an eyebrow raised before bouncing off in the direction of my tattered shelter.

When I turned back to Grey, he was watching me. I felt my shoulders come up in a shrug.

"Do it again," he commanded, and I wondered if I heard a hint of excitement in his voice.

Almost too fast to see, his fist was coming at me once more. It stopped as my palm came up to meet it automatically.

Grey smiled.

My hand still blocking his, he twisted to take my fingers, leading me by the hand as he walked from the center of the temple and farther from the others.

"When did your instincts return, Freya?" he asked in a low voice.

I stared at him, having no idea what he was talking about.

His smile turned apologetic but at the same time unrepentant, an expression I was sure only Grey could get away with. "Seems the wicked Francine is helping you out more than herself."

I shivered at the mention of Fannie. I had plenty of awful

memories of her, cruel as she was, but nothing had compared to the look she'd given me in her panther form. It was only a dream, but the way she'd watched me...

The words came out almost as a thought. "What does she want with me?"

He looked incredulous, but I couldn't understand why. I must have been missing something obvious again. I wondered if she intended to punish me for what I'd done or because of my imagined part in her binding and imprisonment.

Grey turned to me, placing his hands on my arms. "Frey, you are the leader of the North."

I didn't understand what that had to do with it.

He could obviously see that he wasn't getting through. "Do you remember what you read of Francine in the diary?"

I glared. "Has *everyone* read it?"

He ignored my accusation, and I could tell he felt as if he was explaining something to a child. "Francine is in line for the throne, Freya. After you."

Anger flooded through me. There was no betrayal, only fury. "She plans to kill me."

Grey shushed me, but I couldn't be calmed. Fannie had been hunting me down in beast form to kill me. The idea hadn't even crossed my mind. I expected punishment, yes, or some form of prolonged torture, but she wanted to kill me. A hysterical laugh escaped. *For the throne.*

Grey glanced nervously toward the others. They wouldn't want me to know. My fragile brain wouldn't be able to take it.

"Wait... wait," I said. "This doesn't make any sense. Why am I even leader? Why isn't Asher?"

"It doesn't work that way, Frey. The leader can choose the next in his line, but in a conflict, power is the deciding factor."

I was lost again.

He threw another quick glance at the others before he

continued in a hushed tone. "Francine is not as powerful as you are, Frey. You would have to be… out of the picture for her to rule."

"She's stronger than Asher? *I'm* stronger than Asher?"

"She's counting on Council disposing of him." I didn't miss that he'd avoided the other question.

My hands were shaking, so I tried to calm myself before the blackness came. Grey waited, uneasy.

"Why am I the leader? If Asher is alive, why would I be ruler?" My gaze bore into his, forcing him to answer. "Am I stronger than Asher?"

His tone was severe. "No one is stronger than Asher."

That threw me—none of it was making any sense. "Then why?"

"It's very complicated, Frey. Grand Council intends to remove him again—"

I cut him off. "Again?"

"Frey, just…" He trailed off as someone approached then concocted a new conversation. "So you'll want to try and anticipate where I'll strike. Oh hey, Ruby. Are we ready to go?"

I had to work to conceal my growl of irritation, but Ruby was already eyeing me suspiciously.

WE RODE LATE into the evening, and the group became silent as darkness fell. When we finally stopped, we were deep in a forest, thick brush close against our camp. I slid from my horse and found a downed tree to lean against, its bark covered with soft amber-tipped moss. Ruby brought me a blanket, and I watched as she cornered Grey, something I was sure she'd been dying to do since the afternoon's practice.

I had started to doze off when Chevelle sat on the tree beside where my head rested, and I sat up, immediately alert.

"Sleep, Frey."

Unlikely now, I thought, sighing as I tried and failed to settle back in to the comfortable spot I'd been in before. It was a struggle to keep my thoughts from returning to questions about Fannie and Asher, about me. That was possibly the most disturbing part. It was starting to sink in that I was expected to be a ruler and that my throne was something people wanted enough to kill me. I had always disliked Fannie, but it was still hard to believe she would be so utterly ruthless, not that I hadn't wished her dead a few times.

And I didn't understand why it was so important that Asher not be the one to rule. At least he had his mind. But no one knew I didn't. My guard had kept it a secret for my protection.

~

DAWN CAME EARLY. I was wrapped in a blanket near the same fallen tree when Ruby urged me awake with her foot. "Come on, Frey. Time for practice before we move on."

I groaned, but practice was brief because it was only a short time before they were mounted, ready to set off.

We rode too fast, in and out of patches of hot sun and dense forest, the scents and sounds more familiar to my recent memory. The plots of forest were becoming longer, though, and by the evening of the second day, I was getting annoyed with being smacked in the head by so many limbs.

"Wouldn't it just be easier to walk?"

"We are conserving energy," Grey answered in a low voice. "The horses spare us the energy we would have used running while carrying our weapons and packs. We are taking every precaution."

My horse ran into the back of Anvil's as we stopped unexpectedly. I gave him a sheepish grin. He didn't seem surprised that I hadn't been paying attention.

As we stepped down off the horses, Ruby caught sight of all the scrapes and scratches I'd gained from the day's ride. It felt like every branch had hit my face. "You look terrible, Frey." It seemed to delight her to be furnished with a task. She gathered her supplies then cornered me, making repairs for a full hour before she tired of it. She admitted defeat with a sigh. "I shouldn't have let it go so long."

Grey laughed from where he'd been watching her toil beside us, and Ruby sauntered off on some other venture.

I took the opportunity while we were alone. "So how long have you known about Fannie?" I asked, indicating the group.

He only looked back at me.

"I mean, how long has she been stalking me?"

"Not so long," he answered in a hushed tone.

He was glancing around, placing the others, I thought, so I lowered my voice as well. "Is she only using cats?"

"I wouldn't know, Frey. We are simply being... overcautious."

My brow knitted.

"Is there something else?" he asked.

"It just bothers me. The cats, I mean."

He laughed, shifting to rest an elbow on his knee. "They didn't seem to bother you so much at the castle. They are practically sleeping in our beds as we speak."

"That's different," I protested.

"Does it seem so far off that she could have gotten the idea from you? I'm certain your cats are the tale of the North by now."

My eyes narrowed, but having no defense, I shrugged it off, though it did bother me, tremendously.

Suddenly, the atmosphere changed. Grey stiffened, and before I could process the difference, he was gone. In his place stood Ruby, ready in her protective fighting stance.

I tried to stay calm and remember to breathe. I didn't know if it was what we'd been waiting for, Grand Council, or if it was the new threat of Fannie. I realized I was hoping it was the latter. I was standing, ready to face her. I wanted to tear her apart. My anger was staggering.

Then Ruby straightened slightly, relaxing her shoulders and adjusting her belt, but still watching. I followed her gaze to find Junnie. I didn't know how to categorize Junnie, but I didn't think she intended to hurt me, kill me, as Fannie planned, or burn me, as Council wanted.

But I hesitated, because Junnie *was* Council. My ears were ringing in a low buzz as I tried to concentrate. My focus wasn't on the memory of her chasing Asher, on the endless days we'd spent in her study, on her story in my mother's diary, or on the limp body of the human girl. I tried to hone in on what she was saying to Chevelle.

They came closer, and the ringing got louder. It was only a moment before I understood they were stopping me from listening. I didn't waste time being angry with them. I only closed my eyes and moved to the mind of my horse, where there was no ringing to be found.

"No, he is helping her. She's forgotten everything, or maybe she's just using him as well."

I could hear Junnie clearly, but Chevelle was harder to understand—he was speaking so low that the conversation sounded one-sided.

"Apparently, she's decided this was the better path. I doubt she trusts him completely, but for now, they are assisting each other."

Chevelle's face was furious. For a moment, I thought he must have realized I was listening, but he turned away, facing Junnie as he answered, anger bringing out a growl in his muffled voice.

"I don't think he sees it that way," Junnie said. "He may not even know that she's found a side occupation. Regardless, he's not to be trusted."

Chevelle's hand was clenched in a fist at his side—I still couldn't hear him as they spoke, only Junnie. "He's merely using her to eliminate as many of us as possible without risk to him," she said.

Us. I was back in my own head, where spots swirled in blackness. Junnie was Grand Council, and not only was she after Asher, he was after her, And Fannie was after everyone. I tried to stop the swirling, fighting to stay afloat, but by the time I had it under control, Junnie was gone.

The others spoke in guarded tones and clipped words, but I didn't try to decipher what they were planning. My mind was a mess, the strain on the bonds too much. I sat quietly, eyes closed, exhausted from fighting images of Junnie and Fannie and animals slaughtering Council one by one.

When my eyes finally opened again, they found Ruby, ever faithful at my side. She offered me a flagon of water as I considered the disturbing dreams I'd had the night before. I'd been flying overhead, in the mind of a great hawk, peering through the trees, and I'd seen the human girl—not her dead, limp body, but her previous self, the happy, laughing girl Junnie had taken. The girl they'd called Molly. I recalled the fluff of her puppy's lanky frame, now too large as it frolicked in the grass beside her. It seemed odd I would dream of her so close to Junnie's visit.

And then there were the dreams of Asher's voice, as he plotted the use of the humans and the sense of betrayal as he compared them to animals.

There had been more, though, something that hadn't been in the previous dreams. I was running to my mother. Two guards were attempting to stop me from entering her room, and they had the nerve to command me to leave. My eyes narrowed, and my jaw clenched tightly. The girl that I used to be pulled a deep breath through her nose as she drew her sword and killed them both with one swing.

I shuddered.

"Are you all right, Frey?" Ruby's voice was gentle. I tried to give a convincing nod, and she pulled my cloak tighter around me. I wasn't cold. It was actually too warm. I had an irrational urge to throw the thing off, tear everything away.

I spoke instead. "Ruby?"

She smiled. "Yes?"

"How do they find us?"

She looked back at me, confusion written on her face.

"Junnie, Fannie..."

"Oh," she answered, hesitating momentarily. "Frey, I know you're worried about Fannie, but don't be. We have you covered."

"I know. I only mean that Junnie just pops up sometimes."

Ruby didn't answer right away, so I waited, working to seem patient. She saw I wasn't giving up. "I suppose the same way you found the wolves... and the girl," she said.

I drew in a sharp breath. Junnie must have the same abilities as Fannie and me, and surely the same as our mother. Suddenly, I had a thousand questions. "Ruby, if Fannie was unique, why would Asher not want her? Just for her looks?"

"I don't know, Frey. I wasn't around then." Ruby's eyes flicked to Anvil before she caught herself. She made a show of straightening the bottles and jars inside her pack, tucking the flap down neatly before she fastened it. "And your mother's diary was not clear on everything that happened."

No, it wasn't, and there was one particular part that I was suddenly exceedingly curious about. I pushed up to find my pack, but Ruby was faster. She grinned as she handed it to me and stood to leave.

"Thanks, Ruby."

Her departing smile was enchanting.

As soon as she'd turned, I flipped through the pages to the back of the diary, finding the passage I was after.

"YOU'RE BACK." His voice was trembling, feeble. It was my Noble, young no more. He had been waiting here for my return.

He was an outcast of the village. No one believed his tales of magic, the mysterious woman he claimed to meet here. He confessed to spending years trying to find me. He'd thought I was angry with him and that was why I'd not returned. He was afraid to leave this spot in case I were to change my mind and forgive him for whatever he'd done.

I pushed the guilt aside when I recalled why I'd had to come here. For my Freya, to save her. What my father had done to me, to my mother, I would not let him do to her.

I approached the grieving man and reached out to him. As I held his hands, I closed my eyes. I could not watch as I snapped his neck, the way I had with the small boar as my first show of magic to him so long ago. I placated myself by remembering he would soon be gone, his life so short.

I held him until the daylight began to fade then carried his lifeless body into the village. Proof they would be attacked and killed, proof they must fight the elves. It was not hard to incite a riot. They were fearful creatures. I convinced them to raid the castle, gave them direction.

ALL THAT WAS STILL hard to read, but I'd found what I was looking for. My mother had impressed upon the humans to find the castle and attack. She must have kept it a secret from her father. She would have known the danger.

I thought of my dream again, how I had run to her. I could recall the emotions, the betrayal, but there was more. I had thought her ridiculous and hadn't stood by her as Asher condemned her. Yet she had been right. I'd run to her, slain her guards, and... *and what?*

I tried to force the memory, but pain seared through my head, so instead I focused on what I did have: Asher. He was still alive, and he was somehow connected to my group... my guard.

Comprehension came. I knew, not just from reading the diary, but intuitively, what he wanted. Power and control unique enough to ensure his line, his rule. He'd known her child was half human. He'd thought the humans dumb like animals, but he did not know she could control them until she had created an army.

"Frey."

Chevelle's voice startled me. I looked up, but he was staring at the diary on the ground beside me. "It's time to go."

I moved to stand, and he grabbed my arm to help me, a little too forcefully. Before I could protest, I realized I was standing too close to him. The feel of the length of his leg against mine caused a flush to tear through my cheeks. At my expression, he turned, letting me go to hastily direct the others to the horses.

This is it. It's time.

They mounted, and Anvil's massive black horse huffed heavy breaths as they brushed past me. I hurried, jumping into my saddle and nearly over the other side to catch him.

I fell in beside Anvil, who glanced at me suspiciously. "Do you mind if I ask you something?" I asked.

"Probably."

I ignored the teasing. "I was reading my mother's diary, and I was wondering, why would Asher shun Fannie if she could use the animals?"

I expected him to reply in a hushed tone or avoid answering altogether like everyone else. He did neither, instead answering as if he had nothing to hide. "Francine kept her ability a secret not merely from Asher, but from everyone. She was smarter than anyone gave her credit for and paranoid to boot."

I considered her conspiracy theories about High Council and the villagers. In hindsight, they had more substance than I'd imagined.

Then I caught sight of a familiar expression on Anvil's face. It hadn't been familiar before I'd regained part of my memories, but I could see his manner like a reflection all of a sudden.

I'd been impressed when I was younger with the way he'd regarded my grandfather not as though Asher was his ruler, but as if they were equals. Anvil had shown no formality—he was calm and undaunted. He would have never bowed to *Lord* Asher, and I found myself smiling at the memory.

8

IT WASN'T CLEAR HOW THEY'D LEARNED WHERE THE LIGHT ELF Kore was, but I had my suspicions that the information could have come from Junnie, or the usually out of sight Rhys and Rider. Yet there we were, tracking him down and racing toward another confrontation with Council. Ruby had assured me it would not be like before because the council members who'd been involved in my binding had gone into hiding. Whether they were hiding from Fannie or hiding from us, I didn't know.

The absence of a larger force didn't stop the thrill of terror that shot through me or the strange tingle of anticipation that felt as though it belonged to that other me. I would not be the one fighting. I would no longer be allowed to wield a sword against a kneeling tracker to lop off his head. It was different —we would be facing council leaders, men and women whose abilities were far too dangerous to use as practice, or so I'd been told.

My guard intended to find more than just Kore, but infor- mation had been slim. No one on either side could be confident in who to trust, so we only had hope that his death would bring back enough of me that my mind would be recovered and would find its way to unity, safe from fracture.

We barreled through the forest, the trees getting thicker and more closely woven until the horses came to a sudden stop at an oaken barrier. My guard dismounted, Chevelle only glancing over his shoulder at me as he drew his sword from its sheath. He wanted to save the person who was trapped inside of me, the one who wanted to fight. He wanted her back.

I wanted her back too.

The others moved forward, cutting through and leaping over that barrier as Ruby and Steed stood with me.

They watched me, not the forest, obviously waiting for what might happen when another of the bindings that held me together was broken free.

Ruby took my hand and looked into my eyes.

"Stop," I whispered. "You're making me nervous."

She grinned, and then there was a flash of light from within the trees. Scuffling, breaking limbs. Ruby squeezed my hand. It was over that quickly.

"How do you feel?" she asked.

I shook my head. Nothing was different. Nothing had changed.

She frowned, relaxing her grip to straighten the mess of my braid. "No matter," she murmured. "You'll get there."

She'd repaired her work and plaited a new strand by the time the others returned. Chevelle looked to Ruby for confirmation and found only a small shake of her head that meant *no, still not her.*

He slid his sword back into its sheath without another word.

~

WE RODE without event for days, and I finally began to relax into the pattern once more. When we stopped one evening, I sought out Ruby for training, even though I knew I'd regret it after a few lashes of that whip.

She must have been taking it easy on me, though, because I didn't fare too badly, even besting her twice. She cut practice short, prattling something about Grey, and stomped off toward Chevelle. I watched her for a moment, but a chill caught me as I stood motionless. I picked up my pack and found an isolated spot among the trees to change into warmer clothes.

Ruby had taken to tinkering with my garments, so the strings of the vest I held were adorned with tiny beaded jewels and feathers. The latter reminded me of my strategy to sweep the sky each day, which I cringed at neglecting again. I stuffed the bejeweled vest back into the pack, and the next morning, as soon as we mounted, I found a black kite soaring above and closed my eyes, settling into its mind.

Though it had been a cool morning, the sun was bright, and the sky was clear. I could see the landscape far and wide, so it was embarrassing how long I drifted in that hawk before I noticed that something was wrong with the lack of trees and the abundance of rock. I didn't know exactly where we were going, but I had no doubt that wherever the other members of Council were, it wasn't back up the mountain.

I pulled back to my body and almost before I opened my eyes shot out, "Where are we going?"

Five of them turned to me. Ruby said, "Oh."

"Oh?" I repeated.

"Well"—she shrugged—"there was a change of plans."

"And no one thought to tell me."

She smiled. "You just swoon so easily these days, I didn't

know if I should." At the sound of my teeth grinding, her playful tone disappeared. "Frey, please. Trust us."

I narrowed my eyes.

"Fine." She sighed. "We are going back to the castle."

We had been riding for days in the opposite direction, and I'd had no idea. I didn't know what irritated me more, the fact that they'd left me in the dark or that I'd been oblivious. "Wait, *why* are we going back to the castle?"

The horses slowed to a walk, and I could feel the tension surge. I swallowed hard. I really didn't want to swoon so soon after being accused of swooning.

Ruby explained, "Fannie has destroyed a number of Grand Council members. Those who remain are not waiting for her to find them. They have scattered and are too well protected for us to simply stop by for a visit."

I wondered if Council was busy chasing after her, if they had given up on me for the moment. I wondered how many were dead by Fannie's hand, and I asked.

"We do not have an exact count."

"But several. And Ruby, I don't have my mind back." I felt my features contort, and I worked to compose them, not wanting more information kept from me in their attempt to protect me.

"We will take care of you, Frey. We will find those who remain and—"

"Ruby," I interrupted, "why haven't I recovered? How many of them were in on the binding?"

"It's not how many, Frey. It's which ones."

The information caused tumult in my mind, and I had to take a deep breath as I attempted to find order. Fannie was slaughtering Council at random, causing them to scatter or come after her, but we still had to find the right ones, those who had twisted the spell through my mind.

Then I recalled Junnie's part in the ordeal. She'd shown up out of the blue and, it seemed, informed on Fannie. I wondered if she was acting on behalf of Grand Council, trying to get us to stop Fannie's agenda for them, but I'd seen Junnie fighting against Council at that initial battle, before she'd gone after Asher.

My hand tightened on the strap at my waist as my head began to throb, and I had to draw back and blur my focus. It was near impossible, and in the end, I was forced to return to the sky to avoid the commotion of my own mind.

I circled overhead for a while, watching us ride below and contemplating the peculiarity of seeing myself. I started to play a game, jumping from the bird to my body and changing the view from above to below, but the flashes made me dizzy, so I stayed in the bird.

I was flying when I was attacked. Hooks tore into my back, taking feathers with them when they pulled away. The yellow curve of a beak flashed as I was assaulted again, talons tearing into my wings next. I tried to maneuver clear of my aggressor, but it was futile—I was struck again and again, claws tearing out more feathers. I fought to no avail. Somehow, I knew it was the loss of my feathers making it harder to fly, so I relaxed just enough to let the bird have control, hoping its instincts would guide us better than my efforts. We were being thrashed by the attacker, and nothing I could do seemed to be working.

Then I remembered myself. It wasn't my true body being assaulted—it was the bird's. The realization eased the alarm that was building, and I formed a new plan. I jumped to the mind of the other bird, but the second I hit, the tension increased tenfold. The shock threw me back into my mind, and my body jerked in response. I was only trying to breathe, but it came as more of a gasp as my head snapped up to find her in the sky.

"Frey!" Ruby's voice cut through my disbelief, and in an instant, I remembered I wasn't actually in danger.

I *was* incensed, however. My eyes narrowed on my attacker in the blue sky, but before I could pluck her head from her neck, both birds dropped from the sky. I watched them as they plummeted in a tangle, finally landing with a muffled whump on the ground. I had expected a softer touchdown.

I shook my head as I turned to look at the others, who were clearly waiting for an explanation.

"Frey?" Chevelle asked.

I sighed. "I was just up there"—I pointed to the sky for unnecessary emphasis—"and plague strike me, I was mugged."

"That's all?"

"No." I hesitated, but it was almost pointless. They knew so much. "There was someone there. Fannie, I assume."

The group was in an uproar. Confusion and anger eddied around me. Bewildered, I interrupted the commotion. "If you didn't know it was her, why did you drop them?" I asked, indicating the lifeless bodies on the ground.

"I told you, we need to kill all of them," Anvil said, his level words directed at Chevelle.

Chevelle nodded his assent as he looked at me. "No more birds."

He was telling me I couldn't fly. "What? Why?"

"We only left them for you," he said with a hint of regret.

It took a moment before I understood. They had been killing all the animals, leaving nothing but the birds. He wasn't asking me to give them up—he was telling the others to destroy them.

Fannie hadn't hurt me. She'd only irritated me. But she'd gotten my birds taken away. I suppressed a growl.

Chevelle and the others swept our surroundings as they set off again, and I just sat and stared at them. One of them must have noticed, because the horse beneath me took off without my command, nearly tossing me from the saddle before joining the group. I had to restrain myself from riding by crossing my arms, and I glowered intensely. I was tired of feeling helpless and impotent, and I couldn't believe they'd taken my birds.

Anvil was riding beside me, smirking at my scowl. By some means, it made me feel slightly less irritated. I couldn't fathom his effect on me. He was in some of the few memories I had recovered after the battle with Council. I could see him there, his magnetism strong even in a faded recollection.

"You feel familiar with the hawk?" he asked.

The easy question threw me, but I gave a short nod. Anvil smiled, and I tried not to think of the dreams I'd had of burning his tongue and the hawk tearing it out.

"You will be with him again," he assured me, tilting his head slightly as he clicked his heels to join the front of the pack.

I was unnerved for the rest of the day. It was still bothering me when I fell asleep, which was probably what brought on the dream.

I was engulfed in blackness again. I could see the large dark man with the scar and felt nothing but hatred toward him. He was focused not on me, but on something else, a strange lump just beyond my field of vision. I didn't know why, but the lump meant something to me. I concentrated on the dark man's face and grasped the detail that made the difference: there was no scar, not yet. I knew it was coming, though, when out of the periphery came a blinding strike of lightning. The shot was partially deflected by the large man, but it caught his brow, and his previously smug face became enraged. I felt my chest swell just as I heard the laughing response, and though I woke before I could see his massive frame, I knew it came from Anvil.

I SHOT UP, suddenly awake and short of breath, the way I felt when I was roused from the violence of the battle dreams. I surveyed my surroundings, not surprised to find the others watching me with concern. I attempted a weak smile, and most of them returned to their tasks.

I wasn't usually awake that early, so at the very least, my breakfast was warm. Sitting on one of the rocks scattered around the camp, Ruby inquired about my start.

"A dream," I answered. I glanced at Anvil, only a few feet away, as I recalled the dream. Almost without realizing it, I remembered the dark man's name. "It was Anvil. And Rune."

I heard a peculiar noise, and my gaze flicked to Chevelle, whose face had drained of all color. My chest constricted, though I wasn't sure exactly what I'd said wrong. No one spoke.

I could feel the flush in my cheeks. I opened my mouth, but nothing came out. There was nothing to say. I didn't know why he was staring at me like… *like what?*

Finally, Anvil broke the silence. "Ah, my little Freya has been dreaming of me." It was apparent he was going for humor, but no one laughed. He stood, and after a moment, Chevelle turned and left the group. My questioning eyes shifted to Anvil. He forced a smile but said nothing as he walked past me to his horse. I followed as the others mounted their own.

It was a quiet ride that day. Once, something passed between Ruby and Chevelle, but despite the fact that my hearing was better than before, I couldn't understand the whisper. I was afraid to bring it up again, to say something wrong, so I merely watched our surroundings, studying the passing rocks and saying goodbye to the greens and trees. I missed my birds.

We finally stopped for the evening, much later than usual. I was paranoid that it was because of something I'd said, and I had trouble stopping the images of the dream from making a continuous circuit through my thoughts. Steed brought an elk in, though, and I managed distraction for the entire time it cooked and the few short minutes it took me to devour my portion.

After dinner, Chevelle was nowhere to be seen.

I was surprised when the wolves showed up after dark. I lay waiting for sleep when the flicker of the firelight caught their silver fur as they sauntered into the camp. Their eyes roamed over each of us before their massive frames settled onto the ground and they relaxed into sleep.

I felt more secure in their presence, and when the dreams came, they didn't have the mood of nightmares. I felt assured —I was the strong, certain Elfreda that I sometimes knew. She smiled as the cloaks circled, beckoning them. She faced the panther with courage, defying her lord. And she laughed at Rune, fearless in the face of his might, at least until the dream focused again on the mass, the figure that lay on the floor, that he concentrated on. She was powerless to act, suddenly weak. She stared, and the shape took form.

I could see him now, his face contorted in agony. In answer to my wordless plea, there was a flash of light, a surge of electricity, and the torture ceased momentarily. His rigid body eased a fraction, and I was grateful for Anvil intervening and for the broken man, he who signified so much, who lay so near to me.

I choked on the breath I sucked in. My eyes darted around

the camp, seeking Chevelle, but he was nowhere to be found. It was as if I needed to see him, to look upon his face in the flesh, not in the dream, to be positive it was real. But even without seeing, I knew.

Someone approached, and I sat up, shaken, to find it was Anvil. He knelt beside me as he inquired on my condition, and I surprised us both by wrapping my arms around his massive chest in a hug. "Anvil," I gushed, the appreciation pouring through me. He patted my back, and I felt his shoulders come up in a shrug.

I looked behind me to see who he was gesturing to and found Ruby and Chevelle walking toward us. I awkwardly pulled my trembling arms loose and wrapped them around myself. I should have realized Ruby had stepped away from camp when Anvil had come to me.

I'd desperately wanted to find Chevelle moments before, but with him only feet from me, I couldn't bring myself to meet his eyes. The rush of emotion I had felt in the dream was swimming through me, the image of his pained face and besieged body stealing my focus. I forced my mind to accept it so I could function again.

A tear rolled down my cheek, and Ruby was there, brushing it away. She didn't ask what was wrong that time— she just sat beside me and waited. For an instant, I was overwhelmed and clung to her as I had Anvil, but eventually the chaos settled.

It was dawn by that point, and we shared breakfast once more, though I couldn't enjoy it with the ill feeling that had seated itself in the pit of my stomach.

We were back on the horses in short order, and I was sure that we must have been getting close to the castle. Dark-gray rocks spotted the mountain, and the haze was beginning to thicken. We rode through a familiar pass. I slowed as I surveyed the land, trying to shake the eerie feeling that I'd been there before, but it only worsened. I found that I knew what was coming, how the path would curve just so past the jagged rock that slanted toward us, as tall as a dragon, and how the shadows fell in the crevices where the rocks met. I knew all of it.

I'd started to turn almost automatically off our path when Chevelle called to me. I stared back at him, keeping my face deliberately blank, and he explained that we were nearing the castle and I would need to ride amid the group. That was enough to derail me from wherever the impulse had been taking me, and then Ruby rode away from us, picking a slender path that twisted through the dark and spiky rock, and I forgot the idea.

Anvil and Grey had fallen behind me, leaving Steed and Chevelle at the front. I turned to Anvil and asked, "Where's Ruby going?"

"The castle, same as we. She is taking an alternate pass, as it is midday."

He apparently didn't feel the need to clarify further. "Anvil," I said, "*why* is Ruby taking a different way because it's the middle of the day?"

He used an uncharacteristically low tone as his lips twisted into a smirk. "Truth be told, Elfreda, your previous self was not so keen on the fey."

"What do you mean?" I asked.

"It is unfair to place my rendering of the events upon you, but suffice it to say, you dealt with them quite sportingly." His laugh was almost wicked.

The memory that came to mind was not my own, but my mother's. She'd talked in the diary of her father, Asher, killing fey for fun. I felt the blood drain from my face.

Anvil saw my concern. "Do not fret. You have treated Ruby well. It was merely the nefarious you disciplined."

"How?" I asked.

He smiled again. "Rather publicly."

I didn't know whether that was reassuring or not. "Does Ruby know?"

He chuckled. "Everyone knows, I'm afraid."

I felt sick. She couldn't be seen with me.

Grey threw in from behind us, "You know, Freya, Ruby is not the only of us affected by your... aversion."

I spun in my saddle to see him, positive that I would not want to hear what he was planning to tell me but unable to resist. Grey smirked at Anvil as he began his reply, but Chevelle cut him off. "Silence until we are inside the walls."

It was silent until late afternoon, when we arrived at the castle and Dree escorted me to my room.

9

I AWOKE FAMISHED, STRIDING FROM MY ROOM, THROUGH THE maze of corridors, and directly into the dining area. I had no idea how I'd found it.

I was surprised to see Anvil, Grey, Rhys, and Rider there. "Don't you ever sleep?" I asked.

They found my question amusing for some reason and beckoned to me to join them, which I did as soon as I spotted the display of food. They had already eaten and were enjoying drinks, the roar of their laughter increasing with each swig.

The food smelled delicious, and as I selected a piece of meat from one of the trays, I asked, "What are we having?"

"Mountain lion."

I froze mid bite, though I'd received a report on the cats from Dree only hours before. Grey chuckled and offered me a glass of wine. I took it because I was thirsty, but it wasn't long before I found myself matching their pace.

Anvil and Grey began an intense conversation at one end of the table, and I took the opportunity to speak with Rhys and Rider. The wine had loosened me up. "Where are the wolves?"

They smiled in unison, and for a brief moment, I was afraid that was their only reply. However, Rhys answered, "They are enjoying searching the mountains tonight."

I'd wanted to question them more about the wolves ever since I'd been unable to slip into the animals' minds, but I was certain I could not walk that line in my condition, not without giving away too much of my own. "Tell me about them?" I asked, settling on a general inquiry.

Rider said, "Ah, they are incredible beasts, but beasts we do not know. It is said the wolves instead are ancients, some of the very first."

"Ancients? I thought they were all gone." I had read many accounts of the ancients in the village during my studies with Junnie.

"So it is told. Yet you can see their form is not like our own."

"They're elves?"

He smiled gently. "We cannot know. Legend tells the ancients were more powerful than any of record. It is said that upon their thousandth year, they, being too powerful to pass, merely shifted into the minds of the wolves. Others tell that they share the form with the creatures, each together as one."

I felt a crushing pressure on my chest yet knew it was dulled by the wine. I ran a finger over the grain of the table, looking for some way to ground myself, to stay with the conversation. "How?"

"It is said they were twin." He had misunderstood my question, of course, not knowing that I spoke of sharing the animal mind. But the new information was heady. No twins had been born in the elf nations for generations, yet the power of such a thing was known by all.

"And you believe it? You followed them."

"We do not know, Elfreda. We only accept as truth what can be proven. We are loyal to the wolves because they once did us a great deed. And we are loyal to you because the wolves are."

The conversation had taken such a bizarre turn that I was self-conscious, embarrassed at their declaration. "Why be loyal to me? You don't even know me. *I* don't even know me."

Rhys's smile was reassuring. "We do not pledge ourselves blindly, Elfreda."

I withdrew my hand from the table, my cup forgotten, and I had to resist the urge to flutter my fingers. "Wait, you do know me?"

"We... found out."

"Found out?"

Rider leaned forward, resting a forearm on the scarred wood of the table. "While we are faithful to the wolves, we do not offer our lives without certainty. It was a small matter of research."

My head spun. "What do you know?"

"We know of you, Elfreda. We know of your family."

"My family?"

They nodded, neither apparently worried about my tendency to black out during any kind of stressful situation.

"My mother?" I whispered.

"And the others," Rider said.

The others. "Fannie?"

"Yes."

Sidetracked by the disdain on their faces at the mention of her, I asked, "What about Fannie?"

Rhys's eyes, as dark and overcast as a cloudy night, took on a faraway look. "She had been difficult since birth, we are told, a concern from day one. Though her mother tried to care for her, she was a constant disturbance and grew to be a trouble-some child. Rumors flourished that the lord would give up his plan for union with a light one. Upon the birth of the second child, their father merely exacerbated the problem with Francine, showing undoubted preference for Eliza. After a series of regrettable events and a show of your mother's superior power, Francine was passed over, her sister chosen as heir. Certainly, this enflamed her wrath, and after a time, she began to detach from even their mother, Vita."

I was speechless at the easy flow of words describing the horror, though I had read a similar version in my mother's diary.

"Her mother's death was pivotal, though, and it is thought that she meant to resurface and return as a proper lord's daughter. Upon finding her sister's plan to destroy him, she went to their father, exposing the entire plot. At first, he did not trust in Francine, but when confronted with Eliza's journal detailing the plan, he'd no choice but to see it as truth." Rhys straightened, the movement reminding me how still the brothers usually were, and raised one finger. "However, he did not do as she'd expected. Instead of being horrified with his successor's plan to destroy him, he was overjoyed at her power, a matchless power said to be described in her writings. Francine was confounded as he quickly began to form his own plan, which skipped over his only remaining daughter.

"She became incensed. She'd not the power to destroy him and his guard alone, no more than her sister had, but Francine knew Eliza would not accept her now. He'd be expecting Eliza, was aware of her entire design. Francine could only think of one other option. Grand Council."

There was a crushing pressure on my chest as my thoughts ran wild. I'd never even considered why Council had been there. I had merely read that my mother had decided to destroy her father. They'd been circling her, trying to stop her. I'd never realized that Asher wasn't there in those visions.

To think that Fannie, her own sister, had sent them...

I didn't know how long I sat before I saw Chevelle, his face awash with fury. He tried to compose himself when my eyes met his, but as he approached, there was an unmistakable, though unspoken, warning directed at Rhys and Rider. I wondered if that was the reason they were so often separate from the group—not because they were better watchers, but because they would answer whatever I asked. I was fearful for them but also afraid that I had lost their openness and they would tell me no more.

My concern must have been obvious, because when they stood in tandem to excuse themselves, they bowed toward me. "We are here but to serve you, Elfreda." I attempted a smile.

I realized then that Grey and Anvil had grown quiet and that I'd consumed far too much wine. I swayed, resting my head on the table without another glance at them.

Chevelle was silent as he lifted me in his arms and carried me to my bed. He laid me down and brushed the hair from my face.

Then he walked wordlessly from the room.

WHETHER IT WAS the wine or the stories, my dreams were fierce. The fire that surrounded my mother flamed hotter, scorching my skin as I watched her burn. I could see shapes in the flickers, a blaze of deep red curling amongst the orange and amber tongues, and I made out Ruby, the fire fey, dancing in the hideous glow.

The flames blazed in the background of other images, including the screaming, broken bodies as Fannie razed the village, the faces of each council member that she had butchered, the blood spilling from the mouth of the panther as she reaped a terrible revenge, and her knowing eyes finding mine. I saw Junnie, smoldering in the background as she ran, her council colors flowing in the tassels that waved behind her. She wore an unfamiliar dark cloak, and it felt as if she was hiding some threatening mystery. They crackled and popped until, without warning, they were gone, and I was standing in darkness, the chill air stinging my burned skin.

A faint light showed me the face of Rune as he focused on the body before him, the one who writhed in pain and became rigid when the torment redoubled. I stood, helplessly watching, waiting for what I knew was coming, though never quite quickly enough. Finally, I heard the crack, but instead of the strike hitting Rune and gracing him with an eternal scar, the lightning flashed brightly, a painful brilliance that illuminated Chevelle in a way that was not just clear, but lucid. At that moment, I saw him more clearly than I could ever remember, and I knew that he was Rune's son.

THOUGH DRENCHED in sweat and aching everywhere, I awoke with an unexpected calmness—that was, until I realized I was not alone. Chevelle sat on the edge of my bed—trying to wake me or watching me sleep, I wasn't sure. I jerked at the surprise of seeing him, doubled by the shock of the dream, and I was speechless.

He observed me silently for a moment, and when I'd finally retained my bearings, he handed me a drink from the side table. I accepted it gratefully, my hands still trembling.

"You should take better care of yourself," he admonished gently.

He had no way of knowing the cause of my distress, though I couldn't be positive the wine wasn't partially to blame. But I was aware of the reason behind his strong reaction to my other dream, when I'd mentioned his father's name to Anvil, so I wasn't about to tell him. I remembered the color draining from his face that day, and I became paranoid that he would somehow know that I knew, which resulted in a flush. Chevelle stood and swiftly walked from the room, informing me on the way out, without looking back, that I was to meet Ruby in the practice rooms.

Because that's exactly what I need right now.

I crawled out of bed, splashed my face, and attempted to get dressed. I was suffering from the preceding night's festivities, but in truth, that wasn't entirely why I dragged my feet. I wasn't in a hurry to see Ruby, since Anvil had filled me in on my prior issue with the fey, which was apparently causing Ruby problems of her own. I'd been sheltered from the public so they wouldn't recognize that my bonds were still in place, for my own protection, so I hadn't realized she wasn't as free to move about as the others. I wasn't sure how to deal with that, though it wasn't altogether my fault, considering they'd kept so much from me—also ostensibly for my protection— and I was still missing the majority of my memories, such as Rune and Chevelle.

I tried not to let the dream take over my thoughts. Concentrating on lost memories made my head throb and my ears ring, but I couldn't help it—I kept returning to it. Something about it bothered me more than it should have, and it wasn't merely the agony that I'd watched him endure. It was something else, something forgotten.

It felt as though it was right there alongside the anguish of seeing him tormented, the knowledge of his father's identity, and the gratitude toward Anvil for his intervention—a significant truth, just out of reach but adding to my headache. I pushed it away, counting stones in the corridor as I walked to the practice rooms, which to my surprise, I found right away. I had the feeling it was because I'd wanted to avoid Ruby, who stood front and center, impatiently waiting for me.

She saw my state and shook her head, clicking her tongue in disapproval. "Can't you at least *try*?"

I ran my fingers through my hair in an attempt to smooth it, but she wasn't impressed. The way she was looking at me, like it was time for a renovation, actually made me eager for practice. "Ready to get started?" I asked.

She smirked. "Yes, actually. Chevelle asked me to step it up this morning."

My face paled, and Ruby's grin widened. "Prepare yourself, Elfreda."

Before I had a chance to do anything other than cringe, the room lit up in a circle of flames so massive I could not breathe. I struggled for air, wincing as the heat assailed my skin and eyes. I had no notion of where Ruby stood as she taunted me. "React, Frey. Counter."

I had no ideas, no answer to the fire. The circle flared and closed in, advancing at an alarming rate, and still, I stood helpless. Suddenly, the flames disappeared as if they'd never existed.

"Seriously?" Ruby scorned. "What is with you, Frey?"

I was considering telling her when Grey came through the far door. We turned to greet him when, just as he entered, a large, golden mountain lion leapt from the pillars behind him, nearly landing on his back before Grey tossed the beast aside by magic.

"Curse it all, Frey," he complained.

Out of the corner of my eye, I saw Ruby fight a smile as I apologized. "Right. I'll send them away. Sorry."

"Come to watch practice?" Ruby asked him.

"I hear it's going to be a good one," he teased.

"Not so far." Ruby directed an accusing glance my way.

I groaned.

"What happened? I thought you'd been doing well. Heard you'd even bested Red."

Ruby shot him a glare.

"I don't know about that," I said, running a hand over the still-warm sleeve of my shirt. "I just can't think of—" My sentence was cut off. I'd even forgotten I was speaking when the memory came back. I'd been watching Ruby and the affectionate glare she directed at Grey, or maybe it was just being there in the practice rooms, but I remembered. And it had been in the diary. I was nearly positive.

They were both staring at me, waiting on a revelation when I turned from the room. "I have to go lie down," I said in a rush. "I'll come back later."

I ran straight to my room and dug through my pack until I found it, hands shaking as I skimmed the pages for the entry. My fingers ran over my mother's script, the words I had recalled, the words that supported the memory that was calling to me.

Father is already discussing *arranged marriages, even mentioning Rune's son, of all people.*

A flood of heat seemingly ran from the weathered page up my arms as it flushed my neck, my cheeks, overwhelming the thud in my chest. I heard someone behind me. I'd forgotten to close the door in my haste. I threw the book aside and turned, expecting Ruby.

But it wasn't Ruby. The heat drained from my face, surely leaving it colorless, taking my breath and drying my throat as Chevelle stared at the diary on the floor beside me, knowing that he knew that I knew.

He was motionless for an eternity before his eyes made their way to mine. I waited, struck dumb, unsure if I should prevent his explanation, part of me certain I didn't want to know more. As he opened his mouth to speak, I could almost feel the whole memory returning, teasing, as if it would come back if he would only name it.

He closed his eyes as footsteps approached, and the act felt like an apology.

I was unable to look away but regained my breath just before Ruby entered behind him. He took one deep sigh before he opened his eyes and turned to her, giving no explanation, implying that he was waiting on hers.

She faltered, fingers playing over the layers of dyed leather at her waist. "I was just checking on Frey." She was clearly confused, knowing I'd only run from the practice rooms moments before.

It was silent as we waited for his response, my mind running through a thousand scenarios that started with him commanding her to go, allowing us to be alone, him leaving without another word, him turning on me, furious, or the room bursting into flames as Ruby had demonstrated earlier, which seemed like the least painful option.

But none of the visions I'd had prepared me as he faced me and asked, "How are you, Freya?"

My mouth opened to reply but quickly closed again when I realized I'd no idea how to respond. His eyes, as dark as the blackest sapphires, were on mine, waiting, and though I couldn't look away, I knew Ruby's deep-emerald eyes that so resembled mine were as well. Once again, I was lost, fixed on a memory that wouldn't quite develop somewhere within his dark gaze.

Before I could draw it to the surface, Grey was there, summoning Chevelle. At first, Chevelle didn't take his eyes off me, merely raising a hand to dismiss it, but Grey explained, "It is Juniper Fountain."

He dropped his hand, and his face fell slightly in another apology before he reluctantly turned to follow Grey.

I MIGHT HAVE DREAMED OF CHEVELLE, IF I'D KNOWN WHAT TO think or how to feel about the revelations. As it was, he was merely background noise in a strangely calm set of scenes.

I walked from the castle as my former self, draped in a heavy cloak and masked by the darkness of night as I wandered the mountain. And I was me as I walked, still cloaked, through the long corridors of the castle, unable to find my way.

I sat alone in a room, turning a flat stone over and over in my hand, lacing it through my fingers, focusing on it. And then I was outside the castle again in the morning haze, walking from the path just before the great stone that tilted toward the pass like a watchful dragon, curving around between familiar dark-gray patches of rock until I found the entrance.

I bolted upright the moment I awoke, remembering Junnie was there.

I was running from the room and down the corridor before I realized I had no idea where she was. I'd been warned not to leave the safe areas of the castle without escort, so I knew only a section of rooms. I started toward the dining area but turned, heading instead for the room where I'd caught Chevelle with his tall guest before we'd left the castle, briefly thinking it was odd that I'd stored the memory. My footfalls echoed through the stone passageways, their rhythm not slowing until I turned into the doorway. But there was no Junnie, only Ruby, Steed, and Chevelle.

I colored at the sight of him, dropping my head.

Ruby approached. "Feeling better?"

I'd forgotten why I came. I couldn't find my voice.

When I didn't reply, she patted my arm. "Steed, why don't you take Frey to get something to eat. After we're done here, I'll meet you for practice."

I was shuffled from the room, unable to recover until we were walking through the dining room door. I cursed.

"What's that?" Steed asked, laughing as he directed me to a chair at the end of a long rectangular table. He sat across from me, the carved wooden corner between us.

"Junnie," I said. "I wanted to see Junnie."

"She's not here now. She merely stopped in on her way." I clearly wasn't satisfied, so he added, "She passed through only briefly before resuming her course. Grey escorted her from the gates hours ago."

I huffed as a thin, pale servant placed several trays before us. She eyed me in a peculiar way, and I ran my fingers through my hair, convinced I looked frazzled. My hand caught in a tangled braid, remnants of Ruby's handiwork.

"Eat," Steed commanded, sliding a tray toward me.

I should have been hungry, but my stomach was in knots. He was watching me, so I started a conversation that I really didn't have the energy for. "Steed," I began slowly, tracing the lines in the table with the tip of my finger, "Anvil said that I didn't like fey."

He smiled. "It's not that uncommon on the mountain."

"Well, Ruby... she has to hide?"

"Don't worry about Red. She's dealt with it the whole of her life." He had to have seen that the idea didn't console me. "Freya, she had the choice to leave. She enjoys the mountain. And I've never caught sight of an elf she didn't handle for giving her too hard a time." He leaned forward, showing his genuine smile to reassure me.

"But she couldn't ride into the castle with us," I protested.

He hesitated. "That is a different situation, Frey. You see, we are attempting to keep up appearances here to protect you."

Ugh, there it is again.

"It's no secret that once, you would not have befriended one of her kind. It is simply easier this way."

"What would I have done to her before?" I whispered.

He chuckled. "I didn't know you then, but I have known some who did."

I stared blankly as he considered whether to tell me.

When I could see he had decided not to, I stopped him from his planned distraction, stumbling in my hurry to get the words out. "Grey said it was affecting someone besides Ruby."

I saw it had worked. He shook his head and gave a little shrug as he explained, "Anvil was an acquaintance of mine years ago—"

"Anvil?" I interrupted, sure it had been Grey, something to do with his relationship with Ruby.

"He has an impressively wide reaching array of associates. It seems he'd been punished for consorting with the fey."

"I don't get it."

"Do you remember much of Anvil?"

"No," I answered automatically but then corrected myself. "Actually, I remember him more than almost anyone." I shrugged. "But I barely remember anything of anyone, so—"

He held up a hand to stop me. "I'll give you the condensed version." The hand fell to his knee, and he shifted closer. "Anvil had sought the fey for a specific purpose, but before he'd had a chance to explain, you reprimanded him, searing the tongue he'd criticized you with. In your defense, I understand he was quite vulgar."

I was shaking my head, baffled. "I think I remembered that," I said in a rush, "but I didn't know because there was also a hawk and Rune…" I drifted off at the thought of the dark-haired man, but Steed recaptured my attention before I'd gone too far.

"There's that too."

"What?"

"Well, quite honestly, it was a little-believed tale that you'd influence over the hawk of your family's emblem, and in a fit of rage commanded it to attack him. Consequently, though a piece of his tongue was torn out, Anvil proclaimed his fealty to you the moment he'd witnessed your power."

I blushed, remembering that Steed had asked me directly about my ability, and I'd lied. I blurted out another question. "How did it happen *twice*?"

Steed laughed. "That's an interesting one. Apparently, the hawk caught his tongue and tore a piece away. After you settled, he went to the healer and had it stitched up as well as possible. Later, when you'd accepted his allegiance, you were so furious that he'd so blatantly disobeyed you by dealing with the fey that you burnt the exact spot, simply to prove your point."

I felt my brows raise in astonishment. I thought of all the awful stories Ruby had told of the fey and was almost speaking to myself as I asked, "What was he doing with them?" Instantly, I was ashamed that I'd sounded as if I actually did have an aversion to fey.

"Yes, I'd asked the same of him. Odd that someone so faithful would incite such wrath, but he was confident in what he'd done. He believes, still, that had he only the opportunity to explain first, you would have understood."

I waited.

"You see, Frey, it is said that the dust—what is it you called it? Fairy breath?" He smiled. "It is said that the breath of the fey has the ability to grant foresight to some."

I remembered Ruby mentioning foresight, but when I'd dreamt under the intense effects of the dust, I knew that wasn't what I'd seen. "He was trying to see the future?"

Steed shrugged. "I believe the elders had led the notion."

I narrowed my eyes.

"But as I said, I was not here then," he explained, closing the subject.

I was reeling. He watched me patiently, letting me assemble my thoughts.

A movement by the doorway caught my attention, and I was annoyed to see the same servant, sure she was watching us. I shook my head—it irritated me unreasonably.

Steed chuckled. "A bit overwrought?"

I shot him a too-severe glance.

"Was that a threat?" he teased.

I was too cross to think he was funny, but when he lunged at me, sweeping me up from the chair, my breath rushed out of me in a huff, and I found myself laughing as he swung me in head-spinning circles around the huge room. Mid-swing, we caught sight of Ruby leaning against the entryway, her arms crossed as she smirked.

Steed set me down, and I tottered three steps before

regaining my balance. "Merely training," he said to Ruby as she shook her head.

"Well, since it seems you have things fully under control, you might as well continue her training while I grab a bite to eat," she answered.

"Here?" I asked. They gave me that look, but surely there was a reason we had the practice rooms.

"Why not?" Ruby said. "You should be prepared for anything, after all."

I nervously surveyed the room. There were a lot of knives.

I was sorry I'd noticed as the metal started to rattle against the smooth planks of the table. I took a step back, and Steed laughed. When I realized I'd given him the idea, my mouth screwed into a grimace. Ruby joined his laughter, situating herself to better enjoy the show.

The corner of Steed's mouth pulled up slightly, and I cringed as I realized what was coming. He threw me a quick wink just before the first knife barreled toward me.

My impulse was to close my eyes and duck—I had to force myself to counter the move. I flung my hand palm out toward the blade and turned the knife just before it reached me. I gained confidence after my success, but the blade rebounded from the floor as a second one joined it, both flying directly toward me quickly. I focused on pushing them back, flipping the blades toward him, willing them to strike their target. Steed knocked them aside, losing his playful smile as he focused on the others.

The next thing I knew, an assortment of knives was heading directly for me at an alarming rate. I steadied myself, intending to stop them all with one move, when Chevelle's voice broke my concentration. "Are you throwing *knives* at her?"

The blades clattered to the floor as Steed blanched. Ruby

choked on a laugh. I flushed, though I'd not actually been at fault that time.

Ruby, still smiling, stood as she said, "I'll take her to the practice rooms and set her on fire instead."

Chevelle appeared to be in a foul mood. "No. I'll take over."

I didn't understand it had been a dismissal until Ruby winked at me as she turned to go. Steed bumped my side with his elbow on his way past, following her through the door. Throat thick, I forced my gaze to meet Chevelle's, but he wasn't watching me.

He moved to the table, taking a seat opposite our food, and motioned for me to join him. My legs felt like lead, but I obliged.

I sat on his side of the table, leaving a chair between us. It was awkward, but I didn't want him to see my hands tremble or hear how I struggled to breathe. He didn't seem to notice.

The silence built, and as usual, I panicked. "It was kind of my fault. I looked at the knives and—"

My defense of Steed broke off when Chevelle looked up at me. I could see then that he'd not been thinking of my training at all. My mind raced to figure out what could have him so concerned. Too slowly, as always, I recalled seeing him earlier in a tense meeting with Ruby and Steed. I'd been caught so off guard that I'd not noticed the atmosphere. That part of my mind caught up, and before I could stop myself, I asked, "What did Junnie say?"

The question obviously surprised him. After a moment, he nodded and asked in his practiced, careful tone, "You're remembering more?"

Heat bloomed in my cheeks. I could only nod in reply.

"About Council?"

"Oh," I began. "I don't know." I pressed my eyes closed tightly and tried again. "I remembered some of them, mostly

131

just their faces. But the things I'm getting lately"—I blushed —"they are more about... me."

"You?"

"Well, the old me, I guess." His eyes were on me, and I couldn't stop babbling. "And other stuff. I remember Anvil and stones and... and the path." It took all of my strength not to mention Rune, the lightning, and him broken on the floor. Fortunately, no part of me could even consider speaking of the proposed marriage.

He didn't reply as he watched me, but the muscle shifted at his jaw.

"What?" I asked defensively, as if he could somehow read my thoughts.

He shook his head, his tension seeming to ease. "It's just... frustrating."

Automatically, I nodded in agreement. I knew exactly how frustrating it was to have lost the memories, but then what he'd said sank in: *he* was frustrated by it. It was the first time anyone had said such a thing, and I examined the idea, thinking about how my binding had affected him. They'd had to do so much to protect me, all the while taking care of the things that were supposed to be my responsibility and keeping all those secrets. My eyes narrowed briefly, but then I thought of the last of those secrets that had been revealed, the one I'd done my best to avoid thinking about. I wondered if that was the cause of his frustration.

Heat flooded my face before I even had the chance to consider that, before I could think of all those inexplicable looks he'd given me, all the times he'd seemed as if he might reach out to me. I couldn't begin to reclassify all that had passed between us in the months since I'd met—*thought* I'd met him for the first time.

I glanced at Chevelle, sure my flush would have him moving away from me as usual, but he only stared back at me.

That was worse. I swallowed hard, resisting the urge to flutter. "Why are you meeting with Junnie, if she is Grand Council?"

It didn't sound like an accusation, but his brow raised for an instant before he sighed. "It is complicated, Frey."

I gave him a sardonic smirk. *What isn't?*

He reluctantly began, "While Junnie was a leader of Grand Council, she also—"

"What?" I interrupted.

It took him a second to realize what had confused me, and then he was irritated again. "Yes, she was a leader. She does not strictly adhere to their ideas." I shifted, and he held up a hand up to stop me from cutting in again. "She is helping us protect you for many reasons, but you must remember, she is your mother's aunt."

"She's meeting you to protect me?" I'd heard the words so often that they'd begun to have a negative connotation. "So what did she say I needed protection from this time?"

He hesitated, forming an answer. "It is not merely protection. She has her own tasks as well."

"What?" I asked, suddenly brave.

He leaned forward as he answered, and my courage vanished in an instant. "Freya, there is much you do not know."

That much I did know. I swallowed hard. "So Junnie was fighting Council to protect me?" I thought of the battle before I'd regained part of my memories, before I'd learned I'd been intended to rule. She'd fought against her own, but she'd pursued Asher with a vengeance.

"She was protecting you, yes, but she also has issues with the current leaders of Council. I realize that Rhys and Rider

have filled you in on Fannie and the events that led to the..."
His words trailed off as my face paled.

I collected myself, nodding for him to continue.

"Junnie feels that the event was used as an excuse to rout the leadership and cut the defenses of the Northern rule. While she disagreed with the events that had taken place, she kept with you and Fannie in the village to ensure your safety until those who intended harm were located."

I was astonished even though I knew I'd merely gotten the briefest of explanations. "So she left the village because we were safe."

"No. She left when I had taken her place." My mind filled in the words he didn't say: *protecting you.*

I struggled to keep breathing normally, but my head was spinning, my stomach in knots. "Why?"

"She contacted me when the first council elder was killed."

"What?"

"Quinn of Loelle was slain. By an animal."

My reply was choked as I tried to force the disturbing information to settle in the disorder of my mind. A flash of something distracted me, and I glanced to the doorway, but there was no one there. When I looked back, Chevelle was gone.

I didn't realize what had happened until he came back into the room. He must have seen something too, and by the look on his face, it wasn't good.

"What is it?" I asked.

He shook his head, advancing toward me to take my arm and lead me from the room. "I shouldn't have expected to be alone with you."

I was confused until we found the others.

11

CHEVELLE LED ME TO A ROOM I'D NEVER SEEN, AND BEFORE I could register that Rhys and Rider were there with Grey, he started spitting out orders. "Grey, take Frey to Ruby and stay with them." He turned to the others. "Storm must be located. She is likely already outside the walls."

When I finally understood, my stomach dropped. Storm was the pale-skinned servant. She had been watching us.

The others were gone, and Grey had hold of my arm, unspeaking as he rushed me through the corridor. His posture left no doubt as to the gravity of the situation, and I struggled to keep pace as we raced through a part of the castle that was new to me. We turned a dark corner, and he glanced behind us before opening the heavy door to push me through. As he closed it after us, I scanned the room, working to steady my breathing. Ruby was waiting there, calm as she looked to Grey for an explanation.

"Storm," was all he replied, his jaw tight. Ruby's eyes flashed with anger. I stared open-mouthed as she composed herself.

"What is going on?" I asked, voice strained.

"Don't worry, Frey. It's fine," Ruby said in an attempt to reassure me.

I might have snorted.

"How much did Chevelle explain to you?" My brows rose, and she sighed. "He was supposed to be conveying some important information to you?"

I thought back to our conversation. "Um, Junnie and Council. And Fannie."

Ruby shook her head and mumbled, "I knew I should have done it myself." Then, louder, "Exactly what did he say of Fannie?"

Chevelle hadn't actually pointed her out as the attacker, but I answered anyway. "Quinn of Loelle. And then we were interrupted."

"All right," she said. "Sit down."

I swallowed hard as I complied, wondering how much more my mind would take before it shut me down.

Ruby ran a hand over the coiled leather at her side, not unlike the way I'd seen Steed pet a horse. "I am aware that you have been through much, Frey. We have tried to shield you as long as possible, but it is time."

I held every part of me taut, determined to stay the panic.

Ruby said, "So you know about Asher—" My puzzled expression stopped her. "He didn't tell you about Asher?"

I shook my head numbly.

She cursed. "Please enlighten me *precisely* on what you do know."

My mind was in disarray, but I gave her the best summary I could manage.

Ruby was confounded for a moment, apparently unable to decide where to begin. "Right," she said. "So the first thing you need to know is who they were protecting you from." She leaned in as if willing me to remain calm as she spoke in a low and steady tone. "Asher."

I stared blankly back at her. "But that doesn't make any sense. He was at your house. Chevelle was meeting him. He was there..."

She squeezed my shoulder. "Stay with me, Frey. There is a great deal you do not yet know." The turmoil must have been apparent. I thought I was nodding, but I lost focus when I realized why they were hunting Storm and that she was watching for Asher. He had spies in the castle. They were protecting me from him.

A vague notion that I was picking up on things much faster than I used to flashed through my thoughts, and then I fell into Ruby's grip.

"Easy," she said, carefully steadying me in my chair. She sighed. "Enough for now, then. We'll talk more after you rest."

I might have protested, but my head throbbed with pain. I let her lead me to bed, where exhaustion dragged me into sleep.

The murkiness of slumber was broken briefly by a conversation that I couldn't quite grasp. A man's voice sounded foggy and far away. "No, that's not why. Ruby didn't even get that far before she..."

Ruby jumped in, closer to me. "I'm afraid to tell her the rest. She can't seem to bear..."

Then a deep voice came from farther out. "I don't know how... It sickens even me. She'll certainly not be able to tolerate the idea..."

Then I was gone, floating in a wordless dream surrounded by dark stone and jagged, misshapen rocks.

I came awake slowly. The room was quiet and dim as I sat up, rubbing my temples. I ran a palm over my face as if it could wipe away everything. But it didn't. The hand dropped to my lap as I sat, staring blankly—thinking I was alone—for a long moment.

When there was a sound in the darkness across the room from me, I reacted automatically. Someone's body hit the block wall behind them with a solid thud. Only then did I process what had happened, that the noise I'd heard was merely someone clearing their throat and that I had slammed them into the opposite wall.

The room lit brightly as Grey regained his footing, giving me a scowl.

I cursed, adding, "I'm so sorry," before standing to help him. He'd been trying politely to let me know he was in the room, and I'd tossed him against the stone. I was halfway across the space when he stopped me, clearly uninjured.

He shook his head, but I could see a smile working its way through. I flushed, tottering the slightest bit before he closed the distance and steadied me. "I think we should both sit down," he suggested, straightening the leather plate that crossed his chest.

He led me to a set of chairs positioned against the wall below a massive tapestry. The panels hung still, no air moving through the windowless room, and I glanced up at the golden edging before looking back at Grey to ask sheepishly, "Are you all right?"

He smiled, his eyes teasing. "You are one dangerous charge, Freya." My cheeks colored. "Regardless, I am glad your instincts have returned. Are *you* well?"

I nodded, and he raised a brow questioningly. Given that I'd nearly blacked out again, it didn't seem that I truly could be well. "Yes. It's just... so much."

"I understand," he said, and I dropped my head into my hands, wanting to wash it all away, to finally have peace in my own mind.

It was scarcely a moment before the door opened and Steed came in, announcing to Grey that he was needed in the inner chamber.

Grey stood, bowing slightly to me before making a swift retreat. Steed took his place, leaning back into the engraved chair beside me. "Elfreda."

I tried to smile but couldn't pull it off.

He touched my shoulder. "It's all right, Frey."

"It's not," I blurted out before I could compose myself. "Everything is wrong and different and so... *ugh*."

He gave a sympathetic squeeze.

I was suddenly babbling. "I mean, all of a sudden I'm a lord, and I have all these people after me—even my own family— and apparently, I hate fey, and I attacked Anvil, and secrets are everywhere in my dreams, and the one person who I can't even speak to without falling apart is supposed to be my betrothed—"

My hand smacked against my open mouth, cutting off the words. But it was too late. The truth was out.

Steed didn't seem shocked. He was merely watching me with that calm and steady expression.

I lowered my trembling fingers. "You knew?"

Steed shrugged. "It was common knowledge."

I felt the surprise on my face, sure he'd shown far too much interest in me for having been aware that I was betrothed.

He caught my response and leaned forward. A tingle ran up my spine as he explained in a low voice, "You denied him, Freya."

My jaw went slack, and the blood drained from my face. When it all came together, my stomach turned. Steed's hand slid across my back to steady me, and I bit down hard against the torrent in my mind, forcing myself to stay with him.

When I thought I had myself under control, I asked, "Why?" I couldn't fathom why I would deny him. My voice was shaky, and as soon as I'd asked, I wasn't sure I even wanted the answer.

Steed shrugged. "I can't say. I wasn't around then." He grinned with only one side of his mouth and added, "I fancy that he wasn't handsome enough for you."

I felt sick, suddenly wanting nothing more than a subject change. "Where were you?" I asked.

His smile seemed forced. "I don't know exactly when it took place, but I recall hearing about it upon my return." My eyes narrowed and he laughed quietly. "You always have been the best gossip, Elfreda. I was with Grey, I believe."

"Grey?" I asked, sidetracked again.

"Yes." His smile was genuine this time. "I have known Grey for more years than I care to admit. And he has been smitten with Red for nearly as long. It must be so strange for you."

I didn't want to think about it. *Couldn't* think about it. My fingers twisted into the material of my shirt. I wished I had my cloak. "Where were you and Grey?"

"With my father," he answered, fondness plain in his tone. "Grey had shown some interest in the horse trade then."

"He doesn't anymore?" I asked.

"Not since he found Ruby." Steed sighed. "He was lost at his first look into her deep-emerald eyes." He peered into mine as he spoke, and I couldn't be sure whether he was taunting me. "So rare," he said, his voice low.

"Are they?" I asked without meaning to. I'd never seen another besides Ruby's, but I'd just assumed I couldn't remember seeing others. No one in the village had my dark, jeweled eyes, but they hadn't had dark hair, either. Everything about them shone as brightly as their magic. However, the eye color could have been common in the North.

"I've never seen another pair, aside from hers... and yours. But I'd never met your mother."

I nodded automatically, not realizing what we all had in common. We were half-breeds. All the elves I'd seen in the North had brown or black eyes and dark hair. It made me wonder how Fannie had changed, but then I remembered my mother's description of her in the diary, her light features. Thinking out loud, I said, "So, when they bound me, they matched my looks to Fannie's."

"Horrible decision if you ask me," Steed said. I glanced up at him, surprised, and he grinned. "I'm sure I much prefer you raven than hen."

I straightened in my chair. "Steed, the next time Junnie is here, please help me see her. She's all I have."

His expression shifted. He looked as if he wanted to say something.

"Well, except for all of you," I amended, afraid I'd injured his pride.

He began to speak, but the door opened, and both of us turned to see who entered.

"Don't trust me alone with her, then?" Steed teased Ruby.

"You should know by now," she replied, but her humor was only half-hearted.

She pulled up a chair to join us but merely stood beside it, curling her fingers into the ornate railing. The bright scarf tied into her curls seemed out of place in the room. *Ruby* seemed out of place in there. "How do you feel, Frey?"

"Tremendous," I lied.

She glared at me.

"Did you find Storm?"

She hesitated for a moment before shrugging, apparently deciding it was my own fault if I blacked out. "Yes."

"Ruby." I looked her straight in the eye. "Why was she watching us?"

"Maybe she was wondering why you haven't brushed your hair in days."

I rolled my eyes at her then realized what had happened. "Storm was watching me with Steed too, when we talked before we trained."

Ruby cursed under her breath, but her face was smooth again as she looked to Steed. "Anything of consequence?"

Steed shook his head, but I didn't agree. Everything we'd talked about was significant, including my memory loss, my issue with fey, Anvil, the hawk, and Chevelle. I swallowed hard. What I'd discussed with Chevelle was far worse than my conversation with Steed. "Ruby, why was she watching me?" When she didn't answer, I moved to the more important issue. "Who is she reporting to?"

Ruby sighed, probably expecting me to faint when she replied, "Asher."

I knew it. And we'd been speaking of Junnie, her issues with Council, and my concealment in the village, combined with what she'd heard earlier. "Is Junnie in danger?" I asked.

Her expression softened. "No, Freya, be assured that she is not."

"But Asher knows she's protecting me," I argued.

"How would he know that?"

"Because Chevelle and I were—" I stopped because I knew what she'd meant. They had found Storm. I suddenly understood her comment to Steed earlier. She'd been asking if *I* had learned anything of consequence, not Storm. Storm was no longer an issue.

There was a clamor in the corridor, and my gaze found Ruby, but she only stood there as if she didn't hear it.

"Ruby," I said.

"They are simply taking care of a little problem, Frey."

A solid thump that resembled the one I'd heard earlier, when Grey had hit the block wall, sounded outside. I rose, but Ruby put a hand on my shoulder to push me back down. "I promise you, your guard does not need your help."

"They're killing the servants?" I asked.

"Only the ones who warrant it."

My head spun, small spots of bright and dark flashing in my vision. "Maybe I should lie down," I admitted.

They helped me up, leading me to my own room.

DESPITE THE FACT that I'd just napped, I drifted asleep while I waited for my mind to settle. Ruby had stayed with me, sitting beside my bed. I'd been dreaming of Fannie again, destruction and murder, her dark, dangerous cat eyes staring into mine as blood dripped from her muzzle.

The instant I woke, I found the remaining mountain lions inside the castle and snapped their necks where they stood.

My stomach turned, and my breath heaved. Ruby asked if I was well.

"I'm fine," I promised, "only a dream."

"Then sleep, Freya."

But I couldn't. Not anymore. "Ruby, what's going to happen to Fannie?"

"I can't say. She's got her share of tails." Ruby giggled at the remark and amended, "Pursuers."

"What will Junnie do?" I asked.

"Junnie is hard to predict, though I suppose she's got Fannie on the top of her list."

"Why?"

Ruby seemed to be considering whether to tell me. "Well, I

guess you're already lying down," she muttered. She crossed her arms. "For taking out Council."

"But why would she care? Chevelle said that she didn't agree with Council's ideas."

"She doesn't agree with them *on certain points*," Ruby stressed. "Chiefly, that they manipulated events to control the rise of the North. But that doesn't mean she'd see them slain."

"I saw her fighting against them before we got to the castle."

"Only those who attacked you. Some did it for their own reasons, not Council's desire." She moved closer. "I can see you're not grasping the full scope here, Frey. Junnie's *entire* family is on Council."

I drew in a sharp breath. I couldn't understand how I had been so oblivious. I'd known even before I'd left the village that her family had received the calling. "And Fannie's killing them."

"Yes," Ruby answered, "and it is only worse that Junnie is responsible for saving her from your mother's fate, having protected her for those years in the village, though Fannie considers it punishment and entrapment and hungers for revenge."

Her reply had the tone of her fey tales, and I was confident once again that there was truth in all of them. I remembered what Steed had said, that Junnie had merely stopped on her way to warn us. "So is that what Junnie's doing here, searching for Fannie?"

"Not exclusively," Ruby said. "She has many arrows in her quiver."

I recalled the battle again and couldn't help but ask, "Why is she after Asher? If she doesn't agree with Council about suppressing the North's rule, I mean."

"That is an entirely different issue. Junnie is fine with leaving you in charge."

"But not Asher? Why?"

"Freya, there is much you do not know. Sleep now. Tomorrow will turn up soon."

12

I HAD WANTED TO ARGUE WITH RUBY ABOUT SLEEP, BUT I WAS exhausted again, and she'd given me plenty to think about. My thoughts were swimming in the eddy of my mind, and it took a while to sort things out. But before long, they had slowed, and I was in a deep sleep.

My limbs felt heavy as I dreamt, each step a monumental undertaking. I walked forever through the corridors and from the castle, never certain where I should be until finally, I recognized the stones, the distinctive marker on the path, and turned to find the passageway. It was dark and cold inside—it felt abandoned, forsaken. I heard the cry of a prey bird but could not see the sky, merely blackness. The bird called again, screeching more loudly, and it pierced my ears. I tried to find it with my mind to silence it but instead found something foreign. Pain seared my mind, and the shriek became metallic and unbearable.

I drew my hands to my temples, pressing uselessly against them, and suddenly, I wasn't alone. I could feel a presence and heard my name.

"Frey!" Ruby commanded.

My eyes twitched open as a shudder tore through me. *A dream.* Ruby pulled my fists from my head and ordered me to calm down.

When I'd finally relaxed, she asked what was wrong.

"Just a dream," I answered.

"What about, a dragon's lair?"

I knew she'd meant to be sarcastic, but something about it seemed right. "No, only rocks," I said.

"Rocks." She shook her head. "You nearly scared the fire out of me."

I laughed at the odd expression, and my throat was raw. I must have been screaming.

After cleaning up to Ruby's standards, we went down to the dining area for breakfast. Chevelle was waiting for us. His voice was demanding. "Elfreda."

I cringed. "Yes?"

"Why are there dead cats scattered throughout the castle?"

I instantly felt sick again. "Sorry, I forgot."

"Forgot what?" Ruby asked.

"I forgot that I'd left dead cats scattered—"

Chevelle cut me off, taking a step forward. "*Why* are they dead, Frey?"

"Um, no reason, really." They stared at me incredulously, and I said, "A bad dream." It sounded almost like a question.

"Fannie?" Ruby asked in a low voice, probably remembering my inquiry when I'd woken in the night.

I nodded, and they dropped the subject. I doubted Fannie could reach the cats from outside the castle, but the others had no idea it could be done from a distance or that I had done it from farther still.

Grey came in, and Chevelle excused himself not long afterward. Ruby was discussing imaginative training ideas with him when Rhys and Rider found us.

"Good morning, Elfreda." They bowed in tandem, both of them wearing nondescript black cloth draped over the dark leather of their new garb.

They had once made me uneasy, but not anymore. I smiled. "Good morning." Inspiration struck, and I turned to Ruby excitedly. "Why don't Rhys and Rider train me today?"

It was plain she didn't want to agree, but they spoke up before she had the chance to deny me. "It would be our pleasure, Elfreda."

She threw a glance at Grey, who excused himself from the table and hurried from the room. I knew I didn't have much time.

"Can we start now?" They were standing already, not having touched their food, so I amended, "Do you mind?"

"Of course not. It is our honor," Rhys said.

My grin widened, and I rushed from the room, hoping Ruby didn't follow.

"No need to run, Elfreda," Rider laughed when we were clear of the dining area. "You may query us on the way."

"Was it that obvious?" I asked.

He merely smiled. "What is it you wish to know?"

Unprepared, I blurted out the first thing that came to mind. "Tell me about Junnie."

"Juniper Fountain, I presume."

"Yes. Please."

"You are aware of her ties with your mother. What else are you curious about?"

"What she's doing now. I know of her pursuits, but why else, aside from searching, is she here?"

"Ah, I see. You are interested in the new Council."

"Yes," I lied.

Rider tucked a thumb beneath the thick leather vest that covered his chest, keeping pace beside me. "Since the conflict with Grand Council over the issue of northern rule, Juniper—Junnie, as you call her—has detached herself from the group. I assume that you are already aware of her surrender of leadership in order to safeguard you and Francine in the village?"

"Mm-hm."

"Then you know of the sacrifices and hardships she's faced. With the death of her sister, her decision was made, her path sealed."

Rider, who was walking several paces behind us, interrupted. "Elfreda, would you not have Chevelle know of our discourse?"

"No," I answered automatically.

"Then we shall train," he said, directing me into the practice rooms.

I hadn't thought this plan through. I was standing in the open space of the stone-walled room where I'd oft been tortured by fire and whip, facing two powerful silver-haired elves who towered over me. To make matters worse, before we'd even begun, Chevelle rounded the corner to join us. Ruby, smug in her triumph, popped through the second door only moments later.

Rhys, holding a carved wooden staff, announced, "It begins."

I barely had time to let his tone concern me before the staff tilted toward me. I stepped back, stumbling when the stones at my feet shifted. I glanced down, struggling to keep my footing. A crack echoed through the room, the only warning of the flash of light headed for my chest. It would have struck me, but before I had a moment to react, the blow was knocked aside by Chevelle, suddenly between me and the pair of opponents.

Every part of me tingled in warning, even though his fury was not directed at me. "Stop," he said.

Rhys smiled faintly, and for the first time, he looked almost menacing. "You overreact, Vattier. We know her capacity."

"She is bound," Chevelle replied icily.

"You shield her," Rider interjected. "She will not find her potential without cause."

"We have observed her with the others," Rhys said. "She has the faculty when you are absent."

Chevelle took two steps toward him, but before he could react in the way I feared he would, Grey spoke up from the door. "It's true."

I glanced at the others. Though their eyes were on Rhys and Chevelle, it seemed everything hung on Grey's words. To my surprise, Steed had also joined us, standing quietly by the second doorway. He stepped forward as Grey continued, "Her instincts have returned."

I cringed at the memory of flinging him across the room.

The tension in Chevelle's shoulders eased just a fraction, and I breathed again, the worst of this confrontation appearing to be over. "Since the temple," Grey added. Where I had caught his fist during our last practice.

"Why did you keep it from us?" Ruby asked, plainly irritated with him.

The group had gathered closer, and I let myself relax as Grey answered, only in trouble with Ruby at that point. "You knew she was improving. She'd bested you without aim."

Her eyes narrowed on him.

"Besides," he said, "you seem to make her uneasy."

Though Ruby was prepared to argue, Grey persisted, indicating Chevelle with a tip of his head. "But mostly, it's him."

My cheeks went hot, and I wished not for the first time that I had some control over the blushing.

Chevelle watched Grey, and we waited. It felt like an eternity before he finally reacted, glancing briefly at me then walking from the room.

A silence lingered until Grey spoke up. "I mean not to offend you, Elfreda."

"Um, no, not at all," I stammered.

He glanced at Ruby as if to extend his apology, and she sneered back at him. "Then we should carry on," he suggested to Rhys and Rider.

"Wait," I interrupted, not so anxious to resume. "What happened to the floor?" I gestured toward it, no more than the dark, polished stone it had always been. It had been writhing and swelling beneath my feet moments before.

"Merely an illusion," Rider explained.

"And the ball of light?"

He smiled at my term. "Not an illusion. And quite painful, I might add."

I raised a brow at Rhys. "So what's with the staff?" I heard a snicker and turned to glare at Steed, but he was gone. Grey tried to flatten his smile.

"It is merely an instrument to control my focus," Rhys explained.

"Even so," Rider said, "never hurts to have a big stick."

The painfully familiar sound of Ruby's whip unfurling brought me around to face her as she spoke. "Earlier, Grey and I were discussing how helpful it would be to give Frey the experience of a more complete battle."

Understanding her intention, Rider stepped a pace back to open the group, and Grey fell in beside Rhys, making a circle of sorts.

"I mean, even if we make her uneasy," she taunted, "it is not as if we will not be in battle beside her." I ignored the implication, knowing full well I would be no help in a fight. I backed away, concentrating on not getting hurt despite it being next to impossible any time a whip was involved. I thought I might settle for not getting hurt badly.

"Do not think of us, Frey," Grey instructed. "Better still, do not think."

His words were not comforting, but I was, in fact, not thinking when the first strike fired. Ruby's whip cracked not at me but precisely at Grey's face. The split-leather tip would have kissed his cheek had he not vanished a fraction of a second before it made contact.

Before I could draw in a breath, Rhys's staff reached forward and twisted Ruby's whip from her hand. She spun to plant a kick in Rider's chest, but he threw his own strike before she connected. She was flung backward, landing low on her hands and feet like a cat set to pounce. Grey appeared suddenly, hurling his fists forward. I could almost see the force that flew from his hands as it impacted Rhys and Rider's chests, tossing them backward and nearly off their feet.

Someone was behind me, and without the intent to do so, I spun, opening my arms wide to heave the energy to block the assailant. Ruby pitched back, smiling, and only then did I realize I had anticipated her attack. She landed softly, but before I had a chance to speak, I felt it again, coming from behind me. I spun, my hand thrusting beneath the opposite arm just in time. The energy hit Grey's chest and pushed him away as Rhys approached from the side.

The ground came from under my feet.

Heart in my chest, I pushed against the floor with that same force, straightening a hair's breadth before smacking the stone. I was very near regaining my footing when I was struck again. I was unprepared and fell backward only to be shoved by some unseen force to standing.

I could feel the tempo of the fight building, boiling in my

blood. I was facing Rider across a narrow strip of space, and he launched his fist forward with a blast that sizzled across my senses. I knew what was coming for me, and unable to make time to find the others and a safe escape, I threw my own energy out in response. The two collided, and a mere breath in front of me, the air exploded.

"Very nice, Elfreda," Rhys said.

Then my legs collapsed. There were a few snickers as Ruby came to my aid, pulling over a stool for me to sit.

That was when Rhys helped Rider to his feet. "What happened?" I asked, confused.

"You defeated him," Grey explained.

"How?"

"You overpowered him," Ruby said.

I couldn't tell if she was still annoyed or merely stunned. My mind tried to catch up with the mêlée.

"How could I?" I almost whispered.

"What do you mean?" Grey asked.

"I mean, how could I have? I don't have near what anyone else has."

Though my voice was hushed, Rhys answered from where he stood. "Elfreda, you are of the most powerful line in the North."

I stared blankly at him, but Ruby seemed to understand. *Probably because she read the diary*, I thought sourly. "Freya, though you are merely half elf, your mother was of the strongest line of light and dark. The magic that allows their rule may be lesser in you than your kin, but it remains stronger than most"—she glanced at Rider with an apology in her gaze—"others."

I sat silently as her words sank in. My mother's diary had said Asher had taken Vita for her strength and rumor of a unique power. My mother had been chosen as his heir over

Fannie, not merely because of her features, but because Fannie had hidden her gift from him. He'd had Rune train me, even if I couldn't really remember it.

I considered what I'd learned of the events that brought Council to my mother on that unspeakable day, examining the differences in the accounts that hadn't come from Chevelle. Ruby had said the "*rise* of the North," not the rule. And Rhys had called it "the issue of Northern rule." They'd made it sound as if the North had been poised to take over everything before the conflict.

I stopped, chiding myself for having an overactive imagination. But there was also what I'd learned just that morning, when I'd asked Rhys about Junnie. There was a new Council.

"Frey," Ruby said, placing a hand on my shoulder. "Are you all right?"

I didn't think I was. All the training, all that "we're trying to protect you" rubbish, was because people were trying to kill me, and it suddenly made sense.

"Frey?" Ruby questioned again.

"Yeah," I said, forcing a smile. "I think I overdid it. I'm going to go to my room."

"Of course," she replied, moving to come with me.

"No," I assured her. "I'm all right on my own." She didn't look like she agreed, so I said, "Ruby, I just defeated my *guard*."

She was irritated, which made Grey laugh, but when I realized that it was true, my stomach turned. I hurried out before they could see me go pale.

I wandered down the corridors, not fully aware that I was getting lost again until the stone beneath my fingers became too cold, the fires in that part of the castle unlit. Heaving a sigh, I vowed to pay more attention to my surroundings as soon as I found my way back.

After making a few turns this way and that, I eventually

recognized a hallway. I wasn't sure exactly where I was, but I knew I'd seen it before. Heading farther to a narrow, unadorned door, I found it was stuck shut. I glanced down the corridor in both directions, but I didn't have a better idea of where I should go, and it felt right. I pushed against it with magic, and it finally gave, opening into a damp, dark cellar. I flicked a flame over my palm to light the room.

It didn't figure how I'd been so certain a storage cellar was the right door. As I decided to give up and keep walking through the maze of corridors, a thick metal plate caught my eye, leaning against the back wall. I crossed damp stone floor to examine the design embossed in the steel. I reached out to run my fingers over the snake where it seemed to writhe in the beak of a hawk but was suddenly gripping the entire shield, pulling it loose from the gear that lay at its base.

I tossed it aside to stare directly into the mouth of a hidden tunnel.

13

BEFORE I COULD STOP MYSELF, I WAS MOVING THROUGH THE passageway and down the steps. Even with the flame, I couldn't see more than a few paces ahead, but that didn't slow me. I was confident—it was as if my feet knew the way, and I followed them without doubt, stepping faster and faster as I approached whatever lay ahead.

The question of exactly what was there slowed me just before I broke through to sunlight. As I stepped from the passageway, which was shrouded in a dark mass of stones, I grew cautious, surveying the land below. No one was in sight. I glanced behind me in the direction of the outermost castle walls. The entry to the tunnel couldn't even be seen—the boulder masked it. But I knew where it was.

I jumped down to the flat rocks, crouched, and ran toward the path, where I'd be able to pick up speed. I was close. I could feel it.

Then I heard the barely perceptible pad of paws hitting stone, their pace gaining on me, and I stopped. I turned to find a silver wolf with his sharp black eyes on me as he leapt from stone to stone in a full run, showing off his agility. In only a few strong strides, he was to me, his great paws landing with a muffled thump on the rock over the trail. He stared down at me, and though I wasn't precisely afraid, I knew I'd been caught.

I simply stood and looked back at him, both of us as unmoving as the stone surrounding us. Then I heard the others.

Caught. I smirked at the wolf as Chevelle, faster than I would have believed possible, closed the distance between us. He grabbed my arm, spinning me to face him. He began with a few choice expletives and ended with a gravelly, "What were you *thinking?*"

I had no idea how to answer, because I *hadn't* been thinking. I'd only been following some out-of-reach part of me, some forgotten memory. But as I looked into Chevelle's eyes, I didn't even attempt an explanation, because just below the anger, I could see something else: relief. Rhys, Rider, and Grey were watching us, and I couldn't help but glance at them. It caused Chevelle to ease his grasp, though he didn't let go as he turned to escort me back up the path.

I hadn't the slightest notion of how far I'd gone we were walking back to the castle. I was exhausted, though I was unsure whether it was because of the intense practice session or being discovered. Chevelle still had hold of my arm when we accessed the castle through a concealed entryway, and while it wasn't a tunnel, I wondered just how many hidden openings there were.

Ruby was waiting at the door. "Well, no wonder she's uneasy around us," she chided as she spotted his grip on me. His gaze narrowed on her. It was hard to tell if his mood was compounded by her reminder of Grey's comment, or if it was merely because he'd left me alone with my guard and they hadn't guarded me.

I was disappointed when they led me to the dining area because I only wanted to go to bed, but I didn't complain. I sat quietly as a member of the kitchen staff brought out trays full of meat, and when I realized it was a servant I'd never seen before, a replacement for Storm, my stomach twisted. *What had I been thinking?*

Ruby asked, "What is it?"

I became aware that I was shaking my head in disbelief at myself. "I don't know what I was doing. I'm sorry." I swallowed hard.

They stared back at me, mystified, and I kept talking.

"I was just walking and got lost. The next thing I knew, I was outside, and... I'm sorry."

No one spoke.

"I won't do it again," I promised.

Steed chuckled, and Grey shook his head, but they both went back to eating. Ruby stared at me for a minute before grabbing an apple from the tray in front of her, disregarding everything else to examine its smooth red skin. I turned to Chevelle, my gaze restating the apology.

He stared back at me.

I had the feeling that he was about to reach out to me or confess something, but he didn't. When he didn't take his eyes off of me, I flushed and had to turn away. Rhys was pouring wine, and I snatched a glass and downed it before I could think better of it.

It wasn't long before the flow of spirits and food loosened up the atmosphere, and everyone began private conversations. I still felt ill at all that had happened, so I only picked at the food. Drained as I was, I didn't know how much longer I could hang on, but I wasn't about to ask to go to my room, considering that was how it had started in the first place. So I sat quietly beside Chevelle and sipped my wine.

Ruby had moved to converse with Grey and Steed, and the others had started to mill around the room when Chevelle finally stood. Relief washed through me at the thought that I would finally be able to sleep, but when I followed him from the table, he stopped just a few yards away. I ran into him.

"Oh," I said, realizing my tongue was thick.

He steadied me. "Don't you learn?"

He was probably teasing, but I colored at the memory of my last episode with too much wine. "Sorry."

He put his hand under my chin, tilting my face up to meet his gaze. "So you said." My answering smile was quick, and he winced, his words coming out as if he couldn't stop them. "I've missed you, Freya." His voice was low and husky, and I found myself leaning into him, brazen with drink.

I stepped forward, wanting to push him toward the door, but I was off balance. When he tried to secure me, we simply ended up turning enough that I could see the others in the room. I'd forgotten we weren't alone, so I rose up on my toes, putting us in a tangle that was too close as I whispered, "I'm right here."

That was all it took. With a compulsion that seemed so strong that it might have been driven by addiction, he found my lips and drew me against him without regard for anything else. It was hungry and unrelenting, and all I could feel was the warmth of him, the nearness, and a fierce tingle over every surface of my skin. My legs gave way, and though he didn't free his grip in the slightest, he pulled back from the kiss to check my wellbeing.

It sobered me. "Why would I ever have denied you?" I was surprised when I realized I'd spoken aloud and that I hadn't sobered at all.

His face went colorless and expressionless as he dropped me from the embrace.

When my feet hit the floor, I kept a hand on his chest to stabilize myself.

"Who told you that?" he asked.

My eyes inadvertently flicked across the room to Steed before I even realized what I'd done. Chevelle's hand shot backward, and I stared in disbelief as Steed was lifted from the ground and hurled into the far wall. His body crunched.

I stared at Steed as without as much as a glance backward, Chevelle pushed by me and out of the room. Steed was stunned, but judging by everyone else's reaction, not going to die. I spun before good sense could prevent it.

Chevelle was halfway down the corridor, but I caught him easily, seizing his arm when he didn't acknowledge me. He didn't turn and only looked down at me as he waited for me to speak. His face was his stern mask, but his chest rose and fell as if it was an effort to breathe.

"How do you even know someone told me, that it wasn't just something I remembered?" I snapped.

He leaned toward me then, his face painfully close as he answered, "Because that is a memory you would never have."

My grip went limp at the intensity of his response, and the moment I'd released him, he resumed walking. I stared after him. When he reached the end of the corridor and disappeared from view, I finally turned to go back to the dining area. Ruby was watching me from the doorway. I sighed.

"It wasn't intentional, Freya." Ruby patted my shoulder as we returned to the room.

Though Chevelle had never looked away from me when he tossed Steed into the air, I was pretty sure he'd hit his mark. "It looked like it to me," I said.

She laughed. "Not that. That was intentional. And a very

nice strike, if I do say so. I meant that Steed didn't intentionally mislead you. He simply did not know."

I moaned.

Even though I was certain I'd heard bones breaking, everyone including Steed assured me that he would be fine. He didn't seem terribly irritated as he dusted himself off and straightened his clothes. However, finding out that everyone had heard the comment that caused it was about all the humiliation I could stand. "Ruby, will you conduct me to my room, please?"

She laughed. "But you are so much fun when you're crocked, Freya."

I let her have that one, but only because she agreed to let me go.

As we made our way to my room, Ruby asked, "So where exactly *were* you going today?"

"I don't know," I answered honestly. "I just started walking, and the next thing I knew—"

"But why did you go outside?" she persisted.

"I'm not sure," I hedged.

"You mean you were standing in a doorway and didn't think, 'hmm, maybe I shouldn't be doing this. Maybe I shouldn't walk out this sealed door—'"

I cut her off. "Sealed?"

"That's the other thing. How did you break—" She stopped short. "You didn't know the doors were sealed?"

My mouth went dry, and she came to a standstill to narrow her gaze on me. "How did you get out, Frey?"

"I really don't know. There was just this passage, and—"

"Passage?" Her pitch rose. "Where?"

I shrugged. "I was lost when I found it. I was searching for the way back to my room or anything I recognized when I saw the door to the storage room."

She leaned toward me, and I actually felt a spike of fear.

"There was a storage room in the hallway, and I felt like it was right, so I looked under the plate with the bird and the snake. Then I went in. I won't do it again."

I was relieved when her intensity came down a few notches. "A bird and a snake?"

"Yes, a big metal plate with a hawk on it and the snake in its mouth. You've seen it?"

"Yes, I've seen it. It's your crest, Elfreda," she answered caustically. "Plague strike me, did you not think this was important?"

"How was I supposed to know? You don't tell me anything."

"Because you go out like a lame waterbird every time I try."

I wanted to be offended, but she wasn't wrong, so I only glared at her, feeling my jaw tighten. She bit down on her words, as well, but still shook her head as she whirled around and continued toward my room. I managed to stomp behind her a few paces, but my head began to throb. A couple of steps later, I felt my shoulders droop, suddenly too heavy to carry myself through who knew how many more corridors.

"Frey." Ruby was impatient as she stood in my doorway, waiting on me.

I had no idea we'd been so close.

I DIDN'T REMEMBER GOING to sleep, but I couldn't forget my dreams. They were so unreal—not at all like my usual dreams but just as uncomfortable. Ruby and I were arguing. "You didn't tell me," she'd said.

"Yes, well, apparently, I've had some trust issues!" I'd yelled back. The room was spinning around us, filled with anger and bitterness.

Suddenly, Fannie was there, joining in the quarrel, but it wasn't the new Fannie who was set on revenge. It was the old Fannie, the one from our house in the village, cursing me for the mundane and insignificant. When Ruby faded, Fannie attempted to persuade me of her theories of High Council's conspiracies. She was vehement and ferocious as she started to distort, her shape deforming until it resembled a great dog then shifting into a cat. It was not the frightening lion, but a slighter, less menacing version that melted away into the carcass of a snake that curled and writhed as if it lived.

Her words echoed through my mind, disgust evident above all else. *"It must be brought to an end. It is a perversion, brought on by lust for power."* It struck me that although I knew it was her, it didn't sound like the Fannie I'd known, didn't carry her unadorned style. Nor did it sound as if she was speaking of Council.

When Ruby woke me before I was ready, I was a little testy. "What?" I complained. She didn't answer, and when I opened my eyes, ready to convey my grievance, I was surprised to see Chevelle standing beside her. She smiled archly. I sat up too fast, and my head spun. Neither of them reached out to steady me.

When it cleared, I peered up to give at least one of them a dirty look, but something was wrong.

"What is it?" I asked, unease waking me fully.

Chevelle's gaze was level. "We need to know where the storage room is."

"I don't know. I already told Ruby. I was lost when it happened."

"It didn't simply happen, Frey. I need you to tell me everything you can remember about it."

"There was nothing. It was only a plain door in the middle of nowhere. I can't find it again." But then I hesitated because although I didn't know how to find it from inside the castle, I knew where the exit was. I started to stand, and Chevelle pitched back, though I couldn't understand why.

"What are you doing?" Ruby asked right before I toppled forward.

Chevelle caught me, and I groaned. When the dizziness passed, I looked up at him and sighed. "I know how to find it."

"Then tell us," he said.

"I can't. I don't know how to explain it. I just know where it is. From the outside."

Chevelle's hold contracted in the strangest way. "What do you mean, Freya?"

My chest tightened at the endearment, and it took a moment to find my voice. "I mean, I don't know where the storage room is, but I know where the tunnel comes out."

An exceptionally nasty word escaped Ruby's mouth before she pressed it into a thin line.

Chevelle said, "You took a *tunnel* out of the castle?"

"Not on purpose." I wanted to defend myself, but the set of his jaw betrayed his anger, and I started to babble. "It's not like I can remember anything. I thought I was going the right way when I found the storage room. I saw the tunnel, and I don't know what happened. I was just running through it, and once I came outside, I knew where to find the path, and I was almost there when—" My words broke off as I reached the part about being caught.

"Almost where?" Chevelle demanded.

"I don't know. I can't explain it."

Chevelle gave us all a moment before starting again. "We need to know where you were going. Can you tell us where to go from where we found you?"

"No. I'll have to show you."

He shook his head. "No."

"There's no other way," Ruby interjected.

He glared at her. "We don't even know what she's going toward."

"We will all be with her," she argued. "It's got to be sooner or later—"

He cut her off. "Later. It will be later."

As he looked at me, an awareness seemed to dawn that the hold he'd employed to steady me was nearly an embrace. His arms dropped. "Rest, Elfreda." He stepped away but glanced back to add, "Let us know if you recall any other details."

I nodded, sliding my hands behind my back to keep from wringing them. Once he was gone, I slumped onto the bed.

Ruby was fidgeting and restless, a rarity for her.

"What?" I said.

"Nothing, Frey. Rest."

It wasn't long before Grey was at the door, and she practically bolted past him before he stopped her. "What's going on, Ruby?" When she feigned ignorance, he said, "Then I guess I'll be going. I was merely checking on you, since Chevelle informed me not to relieve you of your charge."

She gritted her teeth. "He did, did he?"

He laughed. "That's what I thought."

She'd disappeared before he'd even turned to greet me. "So, Elfreda, what have you done this time?"

I grimaced before confessing, "I got lost and took a hidden passageway outside the castle."

The smile dropped from his face.

"Yeah," I continued, "and I don't really know where I was going. Ruby wants me to show them the way—"

"And Chevelle knows better," he finished.

I nodded, conceding his point. Ruby really did enjoy trouble. It reminded me of her laughter the previous night. "How's Steed?" I asked.

"Fine." His brow shifted. "How are you?"

I answered with a vague gesture.

"You are much improved, aside from the wine, of course. We were all relieved to see your response during training yesterday."

"If only I could get to my mind that way," I groused.

"It won't be long, Frey." I looked at him, confused, and he explained, "You are so close now—only one more to release your bindings."

I straightened. "*What?*"

Before he could answer, we heard bickering in the hall, rapidly approaching our door. Ruby filed into the room, followed by Chevelle, Rhys, and Rider.

"Let's go, Frey," Ruby directed. "It's decided. You will show us the way."

Chevelle's posture was rigid, but he didn't argue. Ruby tossed my shoes at me, so I hastily put them on while she barked out orders. "Grey, go get Steed. Anvil is waiting at the south gate. We leave now."

I didn't understand how Ruby had taken charge of the group until I saw Rhys and Rider's expressions. They had agreed with her. I was certain Grey would go along with her as well, even if he thought it foolish. And if Anvil was already waiting for us, Chevelle must have been the only dissenter.

That was how we found ourselves standing in the middle of the path, waiting for my murky brain to tell me the right direction to take.

Chevelle was so near me that I could barely concentrate, and everyone stood either staring at me while they waited or watching the surrounding rocks as if they might come to life and crush us. It was making me anxious.

I was watching the vulture circling above, about to give up, when the wolves signaled from farther down the path. We started toward them as a group, and then I saw the misshapen boulder that leaned just so over the pass. Everyone but Chevelle kept going as I stopped to examine it.

"What is it?" he asked in a low tone.

"Here," I said, heading off the trail, around a tall rock, and down the hidden path before he could stop me.

"How far?" he asked, glancing back for the others, whom we could only hear from our spot off the path.

"I'm not sure," I said, "but it feels close."

He put a hand on my shoulder. "Wait." Anvil was suddenly behind us, returned from the others on the path ahead. Chevelle turned to him to find the cause of the wolves' call.

"Carrion," Anvil said, but his tone was so off that I almost looked back to see what was wrong. I didn't, though, because I could see the way in.

It took only two more steps to reach it, and Chevelle was in such a solemn discussion with Anvil that he didn't notice me move until I cried out.

I fell back, crashing into Chevelle just as his arms wrapped about me. Then I retched into the rocks at my feet.

The cavern I'd been so familiar with, so eager to find, held nothing more than a pair of ruined corpses. The withered hands of the two bodies curled over their sunken chests, as if they'd died in the midst of some horrible torment

14

I sat in my own bed with Ruby, Chevelle, and Grey anxiously watching me. There hadn't been much discussion once I'd stopped heaving into the stones that surrounded the cavern. They'd simply brought me back and waited for me to regain some semblance of wellbeing. I took a very small sip of water, proud that I could place the cup back on the side table without knocking it to the floor.

"Thanks, Ruby," I said, gesturing at my fresh change of clothes as I leaned onto the pillows. I was certain I had it under control, but then the idea of why she'd had to replace them was back, and—

I sat up suddenly, heaving over the edge of the bed, but there was nothing left to give. They moved closer despite my retching, and I waved them away. *I can do this.* I swallowed hard. "What was that place?"

"I was unaware of it," Chevelle said, his gaze shifting to one of the carved bedposts. "It must have been a site shared with you by Asher."

I knew my features contorted at his reply. I'd not exactly

examined the room, but what I had seen was no mere cave. There had been a well-built chamber just inside and wood-plank doors leading to at least two separate quarters. It was dim, but the stones were smoothed and turned, the space clean except for the blood.

The image of the carcasses rose to the surface, and I couldn't stop myself from seeing the hands again. I didn't know why they were so important, unless it was simply that my subconscious didn't want to see the rest of the of the mangled, torn, destroyed bodies. However, the hands had been intact, the fingers discolored but pale, and caked with dark, dried blood. It had been apparent that one pair was male and the other set was clearly a woman's—they were petite, and I could still see the delicate beaded bracelet that hung undamaged around her tiny wrist.

"Who were they?" I asked.

"Deimos," Chevelle replied tentatively. My chest tightened at the name, but I couldn't understand why. He could see the question in my eyes. "He was a member of Asher's guard."

I steeled myself against the wave of unease. "And the girl?" I asked.

He seemed surprised by my observation. "We do not know."

I was certain there was more to his answer but kept on. "What happened to them?"

He hesitated, and though I was confident I knew, I had to hear him say it. A cool prickle ran over my skin before he said, "It seems to be an animal attack."

A movement at the door made me jump, but it was only Anvil. He gave Chevelle a pointed look, but when Chevelle's gaze returned to me, Anvil stepped closer. His shadow fell over both of us as he placed a hand on Chevelle's shoulder. "I will sit with Freya."

I was sure I'd missed something but couldn't bring myself to question it at the moment. Chevelle eyed me hesitantly but stood, gesturing for Ruby to follow him from the room. Grey gave me a parting nod as he joined them.

I glanced up at Anvil, who seemed distracted. When he finally settled in and saw my curiosity, he only shook his head. "You're driving him crazy."

I blushed.

"Yet it is much improved," he said. "It was exceptionally strange before. You were akin to a child."

I bristled. "Well, it's not exactly easy on my end, either."

He barked a laugh. "I would reason not. You expected naught and found it nonetheless. We expected Lord Freya and got—" He held his hand out toward me in a gesture that he cut short, along with his intended description, at my expression. "Now, now," he explained with a grin, "I mean no offense. It is merely unsettling to meet someone you have known and find they are not at hand."

The word unexpectedly produced the image of the remains, and I shuddered. Anvil leaned closer, but when he reached out to me, his massive hands only revealed what had been so disturbing about the frail, petite fingers in the secret chamber. They had belonged to a woman, a human. Heat rushed up my neck and cheeks, my fists clenched involuntarily, and it took all of my will not to rise from the bed.

Anvil backed up slightly.

"There was a human in the cave," I started, surprised by how composed I sounded in comparison to the way I felt. He didn't respond, but his posture straightened as I continued. "A human was in Asher's secret burrow." My words ended in something like a hiss. I was caught off guard by the course my thoughts had taken. "Why is there a dead human in Asher's hidden chambers?"

"Well now, that's a loaded question."

I forced the flames to remain in my fists, waiting.

He cleared his throat and crossed his arms over his broad chest. "Do you prefer to know why there was a human present, or why she no longer lives? I assume you will only make it through one narrative or the other." When the flames bit at my forearms, he was speaking again. "Then I choose before you receive neither. Asher persists in his design to strengthen his line. A disgrace it is, an abomination."

I watched the disgust on his face with confusion. He wasn't making any sense. *Where were all of these humans coming from? Why would anyone want them? What—*

Suddenly, Anvil's words sank in. They swirled through my mind as the familiar, biting pain returned, along with the ringing background noise behind the repulsive concept. *Strengthen his line.* I felt faint, so I forced myself to focus. "Asher means to breed with the humans."

Anvil nodded once.

Just as my mind formed the notion *because he knows*, the revelations became too much. My head spun, and I had to close my eyes against the flashes of light and dark. I wanted to fight it, to finish the conversation, but it was too hard.

Anvil's voice came soft and low, his fingers brushing my arm. "Rest, girl. You're only fighting yourself now."

I slept, regardless of whether I'd meant to or not. But even in my dreams, my mind refused to accept the idea that Asher knew I could reach inside the mind of a human. So my dreams focused on other minor details.

WHEN I FINALLY OPENED MY eyes, I was staring into Chevelle's deep-blue eyes. I smiled sleepily at him and spoke my first thought aloud. "Your eyes are like your mother's."

The expression on his face clued me in that my dreams had not been insignificant at all. I remembered his mother's eyes. I tried to recall more of her but couldn't see her image through the haze.

"Frey?" Chevelle's words brought me back. He was so close, and he was asking if it was me or her, the old me.

I didn't speak. I merely leaned forward, knowing what would happen if he thought it was her. But I'd been wrong. I'd underestimated him.

He grabbed me roughly and pulled me onto his lap, his face only inches from mine. I could feel his breath on me, coming faster as his eyes rose up to meet my own. My name slipped through his lips in a low moan as they joined with mine, his hands tightening around me. Somehow, we had gotten even closer, and I straddled him on the bed. His touch was overwhelming and consuming.

When I finally recognized the sound of the others approaching the door, my breath caught, and I was surprised to find that I was lying on my back with Chevelle over me, his dark eyes nearly black. He didn't take them off me as his hand flew toward the door, barring them from entry before his mouth returned to my lips and urgently traced the line of my jaw past my ear and down, his kiss opening on the skin of my neck and—

"Frey!" the voice at the door called, but I couldn't find enough interest to take in whose it was. They were insistent, trying to enter the room while my hands frantically searched for the skin beneath Chevelle's shirt. Suddenly, he was pulling me from the bed, and I protested, but something they'd said must have convinced him that it was important enough. I stared at him breathlessly as he composed himself and released the hold on the door. It flew open.

Ruby and Grey rushed in but stopped short. They must have thought something had been wrong, though I couldn't bring myself to imagine what at that precise moment. Their eyes went from Chevelle to me and lingered just a moment before Chevelle barked, "What is it?"

Ruby was apparently speechless, as Grey was the one who explained, "We have word that Brahn has been located."

Chevelle released a long breath and nodded. "We leave at dawn."

"How do we split?" Ruby asked, evidently recovered.

Chevelle turned to me expectantly, and I stared back at him blankly. "Frey?" he demanded.

"What?" I asked, baffled.

The look of sheer disbelief on his face clued me in. He had thought I was her, thought my memories had returned—because I had led him to believe so—and I'd just revealed my deception with one word. My face flushed, and he watched me for only a moment before turning back to Ruby and Grey.

"We should meet with the others," Chevelle said brusquely. He walked from the room without glancing back at me.

I deflated and crumpled onto the bed. Ruby approached, and I sat back up just in time to see Grey stop her. "Go ahead. I'll walk with Frey," he said. Her eyes met his in a silent challenge, but I was on my feet, stepping between them with the intention of speaking up.

When I'd gotten close enough to Ruby to feel the heat radiating off of her, I stepped right past them and through the door in no less of a hurry. Grey laughed quietly as he followed behind me. I didn't look back to see Ruby.

I fell behind Grey as we walked into the room, not especially eager to meet Chevelle again so soon after what I had done. I stared at Grey's feet, keeping as close to him as possible so that Ruby could not grab me for an inquiry, but my head jerked up when I heard Junnie's voice.

She'd been in the midst of a conversation with Chevelle when we entered, and they broke off, turning to greet us. She gave a slight nod and nearly smiled. "Freya, you look well." She glanced at Chevelle and asked, "Have her faculties returned?"

His eyes met mine as he answered, "Her memories are fractured, but her powers are much improved." I found my feet again.

I could feel the questions linger, so I swallowed hard and raised my head as if I wasn't mortified by what I'd just done. It was harder to pull off than I'd expected, and I was suddenly talking without cause. "Have you found Fannie?"

Junnie seemed surprised at the directness of my question but only hesitated a moment before shaking her head. "Merely signs of her."

Signs. "Animal attacks?" I asked.

She nodded, and Chevelle seemed to become uneasy beside her. "I understand you have seen such evidence yourself," she said.

A vision of the human carcass returned, and I had to look away from Junnie. I scanned the room for something else to focus on. Anvil and Rider were staring at me with concern. I was still nodding.

Ruby wound an arm around my waist, and I concentrated on that while they resumed their conversation.

"I have since located only carnage and two stillborn," Junnie explained. "Other than your most recent find, have there been any other indicators?"

"Three servants for certain," Chevelle said, "and four others who could not be verified."

"We have removed those threats," Rider added. "No others remain within the walls."

I floated away from the exchange, scanning the gilded patterns on the edge of a wall hanging. From there, I traced the lines of stone as they spoke, their words merely background noise as I discovered an interesting design on the floor and followed it through the room. I tracked it until it ran under someone's boot, and I trailed up the leather to where it met the dark cloth of pants, upward over a leather weapon belt and fitted shirt, then reaching a strong chin before lingering on lips that I knew. Then I moved upward still, finally reaching his sapphire eyes.

Sapphire. Suddenly, it was right there, the name I'd tried so hard to recall, Chevelle's mother. All that struggle, and there it was. I barked out a laugh.

They turned to stare at me. I attempted a sheepish grin, but that only seemed to make it worse. A minute gesture from Chevelle had Ruby pulling me from the room. I hadn't realized how heavily I'd been leaning on her.

WHEN WE WERE NEARLY to my room, she asked, "Are you going to pieces, Freya?"

"No," I answered, but I didn't recognize my own voice.

We turned through the door, and she led me to the bed, sliding a chair over to sit beside me. "No need to worry. You are in good hands."

Ugh, hands again. I forced myself to concentrate on something else, but my mind didn't get far from the scene before my mouth opened. "Ruby, why would Fannie do such a terrible thing?"

She somehow knew what I meant, but her reply surprised me. "Is it so terrible?"

I stared at her, stunned.

"I cannot say that I'm not satisfied that it is done. Fannie is merely removing the foul... *things* that Asher is producing."

I considered that. I couldn't argue that it didn't make some sense, to Ruby at least, but it was so hard to think of without seeing the bloody mess in the hidden chamber and knowing those had been living beings. I felt my eyes flutter, so I moved forward, or at least sideways, with the conversation. "Why did Fannie go to Council when she discovered my mother's plans?"

Ruby looked puzzled. "I thought that was explained to you?"

I nodded. "But why Council?" I thought of how much I loathed them and how part of them had hunted me down. "Why would she think they would help her?"

She answered in a careful tone, "Grand Council is a birthright." I stared at her. "Oh, you are missing so much." She sighed. "Fannie didn't trust that Council would help her, but she knew that by rule they *must* defend her. The laws of Council have been in place for centuries. Your Vita was a member of Grand Council, as was her family before her. Therefore, by default, Fannie and your mother were also components."

"So Fannie was a member of Grand Council?" I asked.

"Yes." She sounded exasperated.

I gave her an incredulous look.

"Well, she didn't attend meetings or anything," Ruby snapped, "but she had the right to request protection."

"I don't understand," I said. "If they had to protect Fannie, why didn't they protect my mother?"

Ruby nodded. "You see why Junnie took issue with the outcome."

It was getting too complicated. "So Junnie is starting a new Council?"

"Yes, quite skillfully, as a matter of fact."

I wasn't sure about her tone. Chevelle came in and motioned to Ruby, and she leapt from her seat and dashed out of the room, probably to meet with the others to see what she'd missed. I sat up as Chevelle took the chair beside me.

"Are you well?" he asked.

A moment passed before I remembered I'd been escorted from the conference. "Oh, yes. Where's Junnie?"

"She's just departing."

"No," I complained.

He didn't comment, only glanced at the window. I was on my feet and to it in a heartbeat. I scanned the grounds below and finally found her, already too far from the castle. I squinted to see her better. She was being escorted by someone. Grey, I thought. And there was a low, dark mass beside her… A large, black dog.

My chest tightened as she carried on, the animal running contentedly beside her as Grey slowed to turn back toward the castle.

I slid away from the window, resting on the edge of the bed. I knew that dog.

"Freya?" Chevelle leaned close to me.

I looked into his eyes, not even thinking before I spoke. "I remembered your mother's name. Sapphire." His expression was unreadable, until I added, "Like Ruby."

His face changed, as did his entire posture, and his answer came out harsh. "No, not like Ruby."

I drew back, caught off guard by both his reaction and the idea that I'd spoken it aloud. He settled, smoothing his expression with purpose, and I cursed myself, wondering why I couldn't faint when it was convenient. "I can't remember," I defended in a voice near a whisper.

His hand lifted, but he caught himself. "I should tell you," he started.

I waited, my chest constricting as my wide eyes gazed into his.

He took a deep breath of his own. "You said that you recalled Rune, my father."

I nodded, not missing the strain in his last words.

"And you know that Asher was Lord of the North," he continued slowly. "So, you understand that, as such, I—*we* were under his rule."

The tension in my chest sharpened, as if a blade had been forced in, and I clutched it as I absorbed his words. I was backing away from him but couldn't stop myself. My suspicions had been correct—he was working for them. They all were. He reached out and, though I flinched away, caught my wrist to hold me in place. For one terrible moment, I felt as if he would hurt me, but I caught myself because he'd saved me for Asher. My frayed thoughts ran in a thousand directions, wrenching me into pieces.

But he did hurt me. Not how I'd expected, not physically— he hurt me with his final words, spurning in me a fear so deep I didn't truly understand. "Not us, Freya, not my father and myself. We"—he gestured between us—"you and me."

Everyone.

We were slaves to Asher and his will, loyal to the man who tortured my mother, the man who was responsible for this all.

15

I HAD WANTED TO DENY IT, BUT THE TRUTH WAS THERE, AND IT was a painful, all-consuming knowledge. I had no idea how I'd been so blind. Of course we would all have been under his rule, especially me. Asher had acted as my father and had been the Lord of the North. I was his second.

Chevelle's father, Rune, trained my mother and me, ordered by my grandfather. Though I had more blank spots than memories, I knew Rune was a close ally to Asher, so obviously, Chevelle would have been loyal to Asher.

No, not loyal. I couldn't be sure where the thought had come from, but I knew it was true. Chevelle had been under his rule, yes, but not loyally. I didn't know why I couldn't remember the same of myself or how I could be sure of his allegiance but not my own. I recalled the dreams, my memories of his tormented body on the ground as his own father, wearing that malevolent smile, tortured him. Maybe that was why.

Ruby cleared her throat.

I groaned, still raw. She leaned closer, and my eyes flicked open.

"Good, you're awake," she cooed.

I glared at her. "What, Ruby?"

"Tell me what you did to Chevelle last night. He has pushed back our plans and refuses quite sourly to explain why."

I thought past the raw ache of his closing words. "Something about his mother," I muttered.

She eyed me suspiciously. "Yes, well, he is likely sensitive about that, if all the stories are true. And they generally are."

I sat up. "What stories?"

She smiled wickedly. Then her expression grew serious, and her tone was so low I had to strain to hear. "These stories, though widespread, are not told boldly. It is said that Lord Asher was involved, so to flaunt them would assure death."

I felt the slackness of astonishment on my face.

Ruby leaned closer. "Sapphire, Chevelle's mother, was much loved by him, though she was not acknowledged by leadership. She was forced to live outside the kingdom, just as he was required to reside inside the castle with his father. Rune was a hard man, and Chevelle was equally stubborn. Reports of strife began even at a youthful age, and the discord only increased with time. Their distaste for each other did not arrive from one particular incident, but one achieved the breaking point."

My hand rested on my throat as I listened, riveted.

"From that moment, Chevelle declared his division from his father by claiming his mother. He intended to go to her and leave the life that had been set before him."

I was shocked, but Ruby wasn't finished. "Asher was informed and did not interfere, which was highly suspect. But on the day that Chevelle was to depart, he was summoned to the gates." Her expression went cold. "What he found there was the body of his mother, draped in a royal gown, a lifeless beauty, intact but for her eyes. Those striking deep-blue eyes that so mirrored his own"—her voice dropped lower, almost a growl—"had been cleaved from their sockets."

I could feel horror and disgust distort my features, and Ruby nodded in silent agreement. I considered the awfulness of it for a long moment before questions flooded in. I chose one of the less appalling ones. "Why would Asher be involved in something so horrible?"

I saw in her expression that I'd hit the heart of it. She seemed as if she wanted to find a way not to explain, but she'd gone that far already, and when she finally spoke, it was in her careful tone. "Freya," she said, "in all fairness, it is not known that Asher was to blame."

"But—"

She cut me off, holding up a hand. "It is thought so because of several factors, among them Rune's strong reaction. He was openly devastated by the loss, something that would have been an embarrassment to one of his position. Furthermore, he was angered by the display."

"Rune didn't do it? He didn't even know?" I asked, baffled.

"It appeared he did not."

"So what did he do?"

She shook her head. "He held Chevelle responsible."

I was mystified. "Ruby, I don't understand. Why would Asher care if Chevelle left?"

She clenched her jaw, looking as if she would refuse to answer.

"Ruby," I begged.

"It was not Chevelle's leaving that he took issue with, Freya." She leaned forward and placed her hands on my shoulders to steady me. "It was that his second intended to join in the departure."

It took longer than it should have to connect her words with their meanings. When they finally did, I was only able to whisper, "Then we ran?" For a moment, I couldn't help but remember my first real memories of Chevelle, how I'd run from Fannie, from the village, how Council had come after us...

Ruby was shaking her head. "No," she said. "You chose to stay."

"He left me?" I asked, with an unfair hint of resentment.

"No, Freya, he stayed for you."

I saw his crumpled body again, a mass of pain on the floor, and felt the agony of his mother's lifeless body being brought to him as a threat or punishment by those that he had to give allegiance to. *He stayed through that. For me.*

It was quiet for a long while. A torrent of emotion washed through me while my mind tried to sort itself once more. When Ruby finally moved, it was to glance up at Chevelle, who'd been standing near the doorway, watching us. I couldn't say how long he'd been there, but I was sure by his expression that he wasn't aware of our conversation.

I stood, walking to him. Maybe it was simply that my mind was overwhelmed, and maybe it was that I'd been wanting to for so long now, but when I reached him, my arms slid beneath his and around his chest in an embrace that seemed to shock him. He was probably wondering if I had regained the old Elfreda, but I didn't speak a word, only held him until his arms finally relaxed around me in return.

My eyes were shut tightly, but I heard Ruby slip by and close the door behind her.

Chevelle's arms lowered to my waist as he asked in an uneven voice, "What is it, Freya?"

I raised my head from his chest to look into his eyes and had to stop myself from thinking of how blue they were. Leaning in, I pressed my lips lightly to his throat. He pulled me closer, and I lifted to my toes to find his lips for a soft, slow kiss. He let the kiss deepen, but it felt as if he was reserved, uncertain. He had wanted me, I was sure of it. But he was trying so hard to protect me. I pressed harder against him, desperate for his response.

There was no question the moment his restraint broke. My body was overcome with such force that I lost track of my surroundings, aware of only him. Tremors washed through me, and I could not seem to get close enough to him. I was filled with a bottomless, compelling need, and pleasure at each touch, thought, and breath besieged me.

I was lost in him, but not as I had been all the months before. It felt true. There was no doubt it was what I wanted, something every part of me demanded.

The coupling was so intense and consuming that I had no idea whether it had been moments, hours, or days. I lay sleepily in his arms as he placed gentle kisses on my cheek, my neck, my ear...

It must have been the kiss, which brought my full and complete concentration to the place his lips were touching, that caused my dreams to slip back to the deepest depths of my memories. My ears, rounded like my father's, figured prominently as several of my childhood memories played out in my dreams. They were not unpleasant, though that, too, could have been influenced by my mood as I'd drifted to sleep. Even those of Asher were calm and lacked any form of fear. I recalled him at the battle, his mouth moving silently as he stood by, watching. And he was other places, too, whispering chants, focused on the fallen, focused on me. He seemed to grow bigger in each new setting, and I nearly laughed at the vision. The dreams progressed to include Chevelle, and even in my unconscious state, I was interested in seeing the new details that had previously been unknown to me.

So I was irritated when Ruby's sharp voice woke me, stealing the images away. "Wake up, Freya," she urged as she jerked the blankets down.

I sat up, mortified at what she'd see, but I was dressed. And Chevelle was gone.

Ruby was oblivious to my horror. "The boys are meeting downstairs. With any luck, we'll be leaving shortly after."

She smiled, delighted. She had no idea. Chevelle must have prepared things before his meeting, thank decency.

Ruby chose clothes from my wardrobe, cheerily packing them in the case, happy we would finally depart as she'd been hoping. I was still overwhelmed with contented satisfaction from the previous night and couldn't help but feel grateful that she'd shared the story of our past with me. I didn't exactly owe her, but I wanted to help her somehow.

"Ruby?" I asked tentatively.

She turned to me, smiling. I hesitated, and she stepped closer, stopping near the edge of the bed.

I steeled myself. "Don't you want to… to be with Grey?"

She looked startled then laughed. I didn't see what was funny. "You were so serious, Frey. I thought you had some significant dilemma."

"Is it not significant?" I replied, defensive.

She was still smiling as she sat on the bed. "Do you mean is Grey significant? Of course."

I waited.

"Frey, we have been together for ages."

"But not *together*."

She nodded. "There are many reasons for that, none of

which are so solemn as you imply. I do enjoy his company and nearly always have. But I do not enter into a union lightly."

"But Ruby, what happened to you before..." It made me uneasy to speak about her poisoning her own mother. "It won't happen now. You know how to prevent it."

She shook her head. "Silly Freya, I know that. He is as safe from my venom as my whip."

I didn't think anyone was entirely safe from Ruby's whip, but I resisted pointing it out. "Then why?"

"The bond is not so simple among us, Frey. If I were wholly fey, a union would be uncomplicated. The fey joining is easy. Many find themselves with more partners than adversaries at the end of the day." She laughed, folding a gauzy patch of material into the pack. "It is different with the elf blood. Coupling among us would create a strong, enduring bond."

"So?"

"It is not something casual, Frey. It is an attachment that could persist a lifetime. Even if you wanted it broken."

My stomach twisted. I'd known that those who coupled were together for centuries, but I'd never considered that it wasn't by choice.

"I guess you must have lost the memory of those lessons as well." She patted my hand. "Your Vita was a victim of that bond."

Vita had died of grief.

Ruby stared at the tapestries above my bed as she made a thinking face. "Though her bond was weightier. Union with a lord and all." Unexpectedly, she perked up and grinned. "Not to worry. There's plenty of time to decide."

I thought for an instant that I might be sick.

Grey appeared in the doorway and gave a sharp nod to

Ruby before he disappeared again. She grasped my arm and pulled me out of the trance to face her.

"Now, Frey," she demanded, "let's go."

Her tone spoke of the seriousness of the situation, so I followed her as she jumped up to throw boots at me and snatch a cloak from the wardrobe. My pack was over her shoulder when she grabbed my wrist and yanked me from the room, and I began running behind her. We hurried down the corridors to a hidden entrance, and as soon as we stepped outside, I could see that the others, each in their own dark cloaks, were mounted, waiting on us.

When Rhys and Rider saw us, they kicked up their horses and sped from the group to ride ahead with the wolves. I found Chevelle, and he acknowledged me with his eyes, but his face was severe. Ruby threw me onto my horse, and as soon as I'd mounted, all of the horses were moving. Chevelle was to my right, Ruby to my left. Anvil was slightly ahead, and the hooves of Steed and Grey's horses followed closely behind.

We rode hard without interruption across the craggy rocks and away from the safety of the castle walls. The group was silent and alert. I was terrified.

Chevelle stayed near me, and when we finally did stop, he stepped from his horse. In one fluid movement, he pulled me from my own to stand beside him. His face was hard, and I didn't ask the questions that were swimming through my mind. I was sure I didn't want the answers, anyway.

I'd thought it was merely a respite for the horses, but when I realized Steed was directing them back the way we had just come, my optimism sank. Chevelle led me to the cover of a few short, spiky trees, giving me no more than a reassuring nod before Ruby took his place. I watched him with Anvil and the others, the wolves pacing restlessly around their group. I could not hear a word of their discussion.

"What's going on, Ruby?" I whispered.

She responded in kind. "We had received word of Brahn's whereabouts, but the delay in our departure will mean some searching for him. The guard will split on short excursions to hunt without losing the group, while keeping you center."

My stomach tightened. "Won't they need the horses?" I asked as quietly as I could manage.

She shook her head. "From here, we keep on foot for stealth."

I pressed my thoughts into the deepest depths of my mind, silently watching two sets of two rotate searching while the remaining three stayed near me. *The center.*

We had finally reached what we'd been working toward.

Occasionally, the core of the group would move as well, allowing new territory to be scanned, and after a while with no encounters, signs, or anything to speak of, my muscles began to relax, and I settled into a long, uncomfortable resignation.

Once, Chevelle was with me, with Ruby and Grey nearby but watching outward. I leaned into him, finally calm enough to rest. As we sat on the cool stone with my back against the side of his chest and his arm around me, the tightness in my chest released. I almost dozed off, my mind wandering.

I felt the familiar sensation of a bird and fell easily into it, pleased to find it was a hawk. I soared lazily across the sky, the current so mild it barely ruffled a feather. It was so peaceful, so relaxing, to be with the hawk in my mind while my body was safe with Chevelle. I was contemplating how my tension had eased in relation to his proximity when the hawk spotted movement on the ground. It started to turn, but I urged it to stay, focus more clearly on what we were seeing.

Chevelle's hand covered my mouth when I gasped. My eyes flew open, and we stood, his palm pressed against my lips, his other arm wrapped tightly around my waist as Ruby and Grey rushed toward us. I was panting through my nose, and Ruby gave Chevelle a hard glare until he released me.

He spun me around, his eyes commanding an answer.

I tried to steady my breathing as the words rushed from me in the softest voice I could muster. "Fannie. She was running. I didn't know at first, didn't understand. But I saw Brahn behind her. He was after her."

"Where?" Chevelle demanded.

I closed my eyes and concentrated on remembering where I'd been so leisurely flying. They waited, but when my eyes opened and I gave them the best directions I could, they were in motion before I took another breath. The others appeared as we headed toward Fannie and her pursuer.

Chevelle's grip on me was tight as we ran, but he was too fast, and I couldn't keep up with him. Steed came to my other side, grasping my free arm, and they ran in tandem, my feet pulling from the ground to skip steps as I struggled between them. When I started to recognize the area I'd seen from above, one of the wolves called ahead of us. They did not slow, but Chevelle released my arm and moved forward even faster.

Steed kept his hold, and Rhys fell in to Chevelle's place as the others flew past us. They approached a structure of sorts, and suddenly, the field ignited into flame.

I stopped running. Steed and Rhys did not, and my feet began to drag, catching among the rocks and dirt. My legs responded a moment later, but neither Steed nor Rhys seemed to notice. They were focused solely on the battle we were approaching with frightening speed.

I could see Ruby amongst the flames. She was burning several large elves, two of whom I recognized from my nameless memories. Grey was fighting near her, seeming to flick in and out of vision with his swift movements. I searched for Chevelle and found him alongside Anvil, both fighting for entrance to the structure. It had all happened so fast, I'd not had time to even consider fear. When we reached the group, their opposition had been reduced to unresponsive piles scattering the ground.

Chevelle looked back to me before his eyes scanned to find each of the others. Then he visibly braced himself and walked with Anvil through the door, his sword drawn.

We didn't hesitate as we followed them in, but I froze at the scene inside.

The one-room structure was entirely open space, filled with large, lethal elves, Asher's guard. Steed and Rhys still had hold of me, and the others were lined up in front of us. Chevelle and Anvil had their backs directly to me, Rider and Grey were angled slightly away, and Ruby paced impatiently. Her whip was loose at her side, her hand wrapped around the base as she swayed like a snake. Her eyes were flicking to each of the figures in the room and repeatedly to the floor. I followed her gaze and found that a body had already been downed. It was Fannie.

My legs crumpled beneath me, but Steed pulled me to him, securing an arm around my waist as Rhys released his hold and readied his staff. I stared at Fannie's lifeless form on the floor, unable to comprehend what had happened to her. Trembling, I looked up at Steed, but he was not watching me. His eyes were intently directed to the center of the room with such heat that I couldn't help but follow. My legs gave way again when I saw it was Asher, but Steed kept me from collapsing.

I wasn't sure how long we had been standing there, but I didn't think anyone had spoken or moved since our entrance, aside from Ruby's agitated rocking. Tearing my eyes from Asher, I scanned the room again, purposefully avoiding Fannie on the floor, and the pieces started to fall together. We were outnumbered. Both sides were waiting for the first move. I began to size each of them up, wishing I could remember their strengths, and found Brahn, who'd been chasing Fannie. My eyes shot to her body—her corpse—and back to him. He was smug, his sneer a kind of boast.

Before I knew what was happening, I was stepping forward. Steed, caught off guard, struggled to stop me, but I was determined, and I was the first to speak.

"You," I growled to the beast, who seemed for a fraction of a second as shocked as the rest of the room. He quickly recovered, straightening his shoulders, but did not respond. He might have been twice my size.

Chevelle and Steed tried to pull me back, but I stood fast. I saw the symbol of the guard on his chest and wanted to burn him. "You killed Fannie?" I demanded, not recognizing my own voice.

He did not answer, and my hand came up to punish him. The others moved to stop me, my own guard protecting me from my ignorance. I couldn't feel ashamed for my impudence toward someone of his station, someone under the command of my powerful grandfather.

Asher's barking laugh caught everyone's attention. I glared at him, and his hand tightened on his staff. "You forget your place, Elfreda."

"She was your daughter," I hissed.

He shook his head calmly. "No longer. She had turned against me." It was a warning.

Chevelle's voice was low in my ear as he pulled me back once more to plead, "No, Freya."

Asher's gaze flicked to Chevelle then. "Ah, still whispering in her ear, Vattier." He spoke with such disdain I couldn't stop myself from looking back to gauge Chevelle's response. It was cold and hostile.

"She will learn," Asher continued, and I noticed something behind him, a movement of his cloak. I glanced down to see that it was not his own, but a second cloak of the same material, a small figure huddled on the floor behind him. With horror, I recognized what it was by the feel of its mind.

My eyes met Asher's in a moment of disgust, and he smiled as if he had just received the greatest of pleasures. "So it is true," he whispered.

The wind was knocked out of me at my own stupidity. He knew I could enter the minds of humans. How long I had spent fearing him knowing, and I had just given him, without a scrap of resistance, my last secret.

I felt all eyes in the room on me as Asher watched me with open delight. He must have been eager to share with them his new awareness, because he stepped slightly to the side to allow a partial view of the woman behind him. There was an intake of breath as they all registered what I had already seen: a human. Then they looked back at me appraisingly, finally understanding the exchange.

"You'll not have her," Chevelle warned, stirring the entire room back to readiness.

Asher laughed again. "You'll not stop me."

He raised his staff a fraction of an inch, and the whole room went still.

I had no idea what he was doing, but I couldn't take my

eyes off the human behind him. Her eyes were on me, too, wide and terrified, and I saw that they were nearly the same soft brown as her hair, which could be seen beneath the over-sized hood of her cloak. Her skin was pale, and she was unquestionably weary, but there was something else, something that didn't seem right. I just couldn't place exactly what. Humans were odd, but this one seemed wrong.

I felt Asher's eyes on me and glanced up to see that he was still smiling as the room remained motionless. It was as if, for once, the world was working at the same pace as my mind. I was trying to understand what was happening around me, how it would turn out, what I should do, if I would scream when they burned me. Suddenly, my eyes were back on the woman. She was clutching her stomach, holding herself protectively. She was swollen with child.

Flames flew from my hands before I could stop them. My eyes bored into Asher's, focused on my strike, and he remained smiling a confident, unpleasant smile.

The fire I'd thrown at him might have been the strongest I'd ever produced, but it fell short. He had barely twitched to deflect it, and I could already feel the drain it had caused me. The anger waned, and I suddenly understood the gravity of the situation. I understood everything.

I knew why Fannie's body lay on the ground before us. She'd been the animal that had mutilated the bodies of the human and the elf they had named Deimos. He'd been Asher's guard, and he'd been minding the human, who was essentially a broodmare, just as the unfortunate woman who was now cowering behind Asher was. Her beseeching eyes were still on me.

Asher had killed his own daughter for slaughtering his children, his half-bred offspring that she'd thought a perversion. I couldn't place my feelings for Fannie now. She'd had a cruel life, and though she'd been instrumental in my mother's death, I couldn't say it was truly her fault. She'd tried then to prevent the horror she knew was coming, and in the end, she'd stood alone against her father to stop what all of us abhorred. But she was gone, at his hand.

I knew then that he'd planned it, the slaughter of Council by my guard. He'd wanted it not merely because they intended to stop him—he'd had another agenda. I could see him there at the battle, the spellcaster whispering chants at the edge of notice until Junnie pursued him. I recognized why Ruby had owned a book on magic and remembered how she had spoken of stealing someone's power by taking their life, releasing their energy to use as one's own. *All of this in his quest for power.*

But that wasn't all, and I knew that too. I recalled Grey's words, and it further sickened me that they had all known that there would only be one outcome. They had known that every move they made would bring us all to this one moment, and that I would never be whole without it. Asher was the final remaining captor of my mind, and he had no intention of freeing me. *One more to release my bonds.*

Maybe it was the anticipation of battle that had sharpened my mind. Maybe it was Asher's presence. Maybe I'd been so blind to it all along because I'd not wanted to face it, but it was all suddenly there. We were defeated. My guard stood frozen because they too knew that they could not defeat Asher. He was too powerful for any of us, possibly too powerful for all of us, and his guard stood before him.

I glanced at each of Asher's guard again. Separately, they could have been overcome. Their confidence came not from an assurance that they could top any of us, but that they didn't need to. As illustrated by the brief encounter outside, my guard was not easily conquered. If not for Asher, they would overwhelm this impressive group nearly as quickly. But there *was* Asher, and he watched me as I considered, knowing he had me and that I would find no way out.

He would take me in and use me to regain his rule. He would succeed. Many of the Council were already dead, and he would finish it. I could feel the memories tugging at me, and I knew he would be a cruel leader. He would exploit my ability, continuing to make new offspring in hopes of gaining a more unique power. He would slowly steal those who were dear to me. Chevelle. Ruby. All of them.

He was quicker and more powerful than any of us. A move against him would be instant death—I knew that. We all did. And yet my guard stood with me, as if there was a chance. It was sad that they had so much faith in me. I was no more than a pawn in Asher's game. What could I do except—

I stopped cold, feeling the smile crawl from one side of my lips to the other.

I had the pleasure of seeing confusion cross Asher's face before I closed my eyes and sank, deeply and swiftly, into the mind of the small, brown-eyed girl at his feet. He had protected himself from us, but not from her. *Not from the piteous human.*

Her hand sped to the sheath at his waist then plunged his dagger into his heart.

The woman's scream threw me back to my own mind, and my eyes flickered open to see chaos. I was standing in the middle of a war, staring at Asher's body, which had landed in the trembling, bloodied hands of the fragile woman. She stared at him, her mouth still open but silent. I gazed into his eyes and knew that he was proud. Somehow, he was in awe of me, that I had defeated him. He'd been foolish to forget the human—he'd thought her as insignificant as a witless animal, and he hadn't protected himself from her. He smiled at me, and then his mouth moved in a silent chant.

As the life slipped from his body, I felt sudden, intense pain in my own. It became excruciating, and I nearly lost the capacity to breathe, but it crested as the icy heat of power rushed through me. It wasn't solely my energy coursing through me—I could feel Asher, the strength of his line, the depth of his magic, and the power that allowed his rule. I was overwhelmed, a torrent of violence and pleasure sweeping through me, almost knocking me from my feet. A deluge of memories, thoughts, and emotions followed, flowing together and joining with the agony and bliss.

And then the storm was over.

I had my mind back.

Although my inner conflict remained, it was not the painful tumult it had been. It was two sets of ideas, as if I was merely undecided. I looked around, disoriented.

Bodies were strewn on the ground around me. The circle of clear floor where I stood seemed to be the only area not destroyed. The downed bodies were my guard—no, Asher's guard. The blank, dead eyes of Eris, whom I had liked, looked back at me from the ground as blood leaked slowly from the corner of his mouth. A few feet beside him, in what might have been two separate pieces, was Domnal. Three of the bodies were burned beyond identification. Near the back wall, I saw Cleve, his form intact but lifeless nonetheless. I wondered if Dunn was among them, and Aren.

I saw Anvil, kneeling in what I feared was injury, but it was not. He was silently saluting me. I found a smile for him. I continued scanning the room and bristled for a moment when I saw a fey, but it was Ruby. *My Ruby.* She seemed to be smoldering. I nearly shook my head in disbelief but resisted. Rhys and Rider watched me from behind her, their robes in tatters, and I nodded my respect. Sitting proudly in front of them were my old friends, Finn and Keaton. I smiled at their knowing eyes, trimmed in a beautiful silver fur. Nearby was the handsome Steed, clearly staggered as he stared back at me. I gave him a quick wink before I searched for who else had been left standing. Grey was undamaged. And beside me, though a few paces back, I found Chevelle's eyes scrutinizing me.

My Chevelle. I knew him in both sets of memories. He'd been there for it all, and I was irrevocably tied to him.

I looked away. Asher still lay in the arms of the human. I took a step forward, and she gave a little whimper as she jerked a hand to protect her stomach. I sighed. Through all the time I had spent wishing to get my memory back, I had known. Somewhere in the mess of my mind, I'd understood that acquiring the magic and memories would not release me from the difficulties of my life. That was the third and final thing I'd always been certain of.

But I wasn't Freya anymore.

I was Elfreda, Lord of the North.

THE STORY CONTINUES...

Please look for book three in the Frey Saga: *Rise of the Seven*

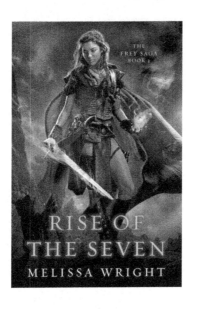

Visit the author on the web at

www.melissa-wright.com

Made in the USA
Middletown, DE
14 June 2022

67154095R00119